CHRISTMAS ROMANCES

FIVE SHORT STORIES

Written by C. L. Hamilton

DEDICATION

I dedicate this book to those who have a special place in my heart.
Your friendship means a lot to me.   Christmas is a time to share your
love with others and embracc their love in return.

CONTENTS

Short Stories

SHORT STORY 1

SINGLE RED ROSE

Contemporary Christmas Romance

Written By C. L. Hamilton

C. L. Hamilton

1. SINGLE RED ROSE

The past is always lurking in the shadows waiting for the right moment to reveal itself. Every year, Kelly made the trip home to spend Christmas with her family but this year would turn out differently. Kelly straightened her aching back as she stepped off the bus into the open arms of her parents. The pain returned when she crammed herself next to her luggage in the backseat of her mother's hatchback. *It has been twelve months since my last visit. This rural town hasn't changed in the last fifteen years.* Old timber shops are still branded with their 1920s faded sign overhead. The original families still owned some shops; others sat vacant plastered in 'For Lease' signs. Desperate landlords tried to spruce up the old shops with tinsel and cardboard wreaths. There had been a few seasonal storms in the area but the country was still dry with varying shades of brown.

Clambering out of the car she faced the sun, stretching her tight muscles and taking a deep breath. The open laid-back lifestyle of the bush was a relief after living in the bustle of the city. With a suitcase in each hand, she walked the same path as every other year. The old Queenslander home hadn't changed. Faded white timber cladding carried the stains of the rusted roof gutter overhead. She dropped her bags in her old bedroom.

It is Christmas Eve, all the action is at the local pub. Why slave at cooking a festive dinner in the stifling summer heat when you can pay someone else to do it?

Kelly sat across from her family in the restaurant. She scanned the room, some old faces seemed familiar but she couldn't place them. The timber dance floor was bouncing with rock music. Strings of Christmas lights created a collage of colour on the dancing crowd.

She rose facing her parents, "I'm getting a drink, what do you want?"

"Cold water and a beer," her mother replied. *They have been together that long Dad doesn't bother replying because Mum always beats him to the answer.*

Standing at the bar a familiar voice came from behind, "Kelly." She turned to see two school girlfriends dressed more seductively than last year. Friendly hugs and smiles lifted her Christmas mood.

She placed her parents' drinks on the table, "Deb and Sal are here, I'll be on the dance floor."

Kelly bobbed away with her old girlfriends. She shuffled around when someone caught her eye; taking another turn to make sure. He was tall with dark hair and there was something familiar about him. Coming face to face, those hazel eyes stirred an old fire within. "Brett?"

"Kelly, it's been a while," he stepped closer and his dancing matched her every move. "Are you here for Christmas?"

"Yeah, visiting my folks."

"Same."

All her focus was on him as moved as one. Her girlfriends were left to do their own thing. *He has buffed out since high school. That weird haircut had been replaced with a short back and sides.* The image of the class all together for their annual school photo filled her mind. *We had some odd fashions back then. I wonder if he is still with his old girlfriend.*

Onto the third song, she stared back into his eyes as he slipped his arms around her waist drawing her closer. Her pulse quickened as she rested her arms on his shoulders as they swayed to the music. *Feel those biceps. He has buffed out.* The last song was upbeat, trying to keep up with him was tiring. She took a deep breath, sweat beaded on her brow and her mouth was dry. She leaned over to his ear, "I need a drink." It didn't take long for him to join her at the bar.

"What are you having?" The bartender asked.

"Rum and coke," she replied.

"And a scotch on the rocks," he placed twenty dollars on the bar. "My shout."

The dance music boomed across the pub, "Let's go out to the beer garden." Brett guided her through the crowd with his hand lightly resting on her back.

It was quieter outside and the green plants broke up the dusty brown boards. Placing her drink on the table, she panned the area. "I need to go to the ladies."

She came out of the cubicle tucking in her shirt when she received a sharp whack from behind. *Watch it.* Partway turning around, she received a bigger shove into the wall. Kelly's vision was full of the woman's head covered with a mop of red hair. Her piercing eyes glared back at Kelly. *What is with this crazy cow?* "What—"

"Keep your hands off my husband," the woman yelled.

"I didn't know—"

"Don't lie," the hard swing of the woman's palm stung Kelly's cheek. The woman's breath stunk of alcohol and cigarette smoke.

Get out of my face bitch. Kelly clenched her jaw as she shoved the woman back. Taking a step sideways she headed for the door. The woman screamed as she lunged forward swinging her fist, her bony knuckles connecting with Kelly's nose. She raised her arms over her face as she pushed for the door. Her pulse raced as everything told her to run.

Another woman walked into the changing room as Kelly left. She hid around the corner, gasping for air as she reached up to her face. Looking back at her hand, a smear of blood stained her palm. *I'm bleeding. What the hell was that about?* She ducked into the shadows as the attacker staggered out the back door. She returned to the bathroom to check the damage in the mirror. A trickle of blood came from her nose and her hair was in a mess. Grabbing some hand towel, she held it under her nose. Taking a few deep breaths, she tried to get her pulse back to normal.

Staring back at her image in the mirror she tried to make sense of the last few minutes. *He's married? He seemed very single. Why the hell is he married to a nutter like her?* She cleaned her face and tried to regain her composure. On leaving the change room she looked across the beer garden to Brett sitting alone. *I can't leave him hanging.* Her eyes darted around the garden looking for the woman that just attacked her. *I'm not hanging around here.* She hurried back to her girlfriend's table and grabbed her jacket.

"What happened?" Deb asked. Kelly said nothing as she hastened out the door.

Kelly was chased down the street by her girlfriends, "Kelly, stop."

Finally catching her they blocked her path. Their eyes widened seeing the blood on the tissue, "Did he hit you?"

"No, his crazed wife. She attacked me in the bathroom."

They looked back stunned. "What's her name? We will go to the police," Sal said.

"I don't know. Why don't you ask him?" Kelly wiped her nose again, "Go together so you can defend yourself when she comes back."

Later that night, Kelly was back at her parent's house relaxing after a shower. When her friends knocked on the door. The family was heading to bed, so Kelly ushered Deb and Sal onto the veranda. The girls were still hyped up from the evening.

"We gave him a piece of our minds. I told him to control his wife." Deb leaned closer, smelling of alcohol, "And I told him you didn't want anything to do with him anymore."

"I wouldn't have gone that far," Kelly dropped into a chair.

Sal leaned back on the veranda column, "Well, he's claiming he doesn't have a wife."

I hope they didn't beat him up. Kelly reclined in the seat, dropping her head back against the wall. "Let's just forget the whole thing. It's Christmas."

The lights were out in the rest of the house, everyone had gone to bed. Kelly lay in her old bedroom staring back at the old rock posters peeling off the wall from her teenage years. Memories of Brett's smile came back. *He had a girlfriend at school but she wasn't a redhead. Where did he find this nutcase? Why did I have to move away to university? He could have married me. I wouldn't have attacked anyone in the bathroom.* Her phone buzzed. *An unknown mobile phone number.* She let it go to the message bank. It rang once more. She ignored it again.

The following morning Kelly enjoyed Christmas breakfast with her family around the outdoor entertaining table. Someone walking up the back garden path caught her eye. Brett stood beside the outdoor laundry, "Kelly can we talk?" His voice was softer than last night.

Kelly scanned the horizon before grabbing his arm and darting into the laundry. Pushing him back to the wall. "You didn't tell me you had a psycho wife." She glanced over her shoulder, "What are you doing here? Trying to get us all killed."

"Calm down. I don't have a wife." His eyes roamed over her face, "Are you OK?" He reached up to check the bruise on her cheek, "I have no idea who attacked you but I had nothing to do with it."

"Well, who the hell is she? You are the only guy I have spoken to since I have been here." She stepped back leaning on the washing machine.

He moved closer, "I don't know." Taking hold of her hands, "I feel bad about what happened last night. Will you join me for dinner tonight at my folks?"

His folks are friendly, they remembered me from school. He has more relatives than I remember, four brothers. Kelly looked nervously across the table. He smiled as his eyes connected with hers. A heat built inside her as she dropped her gaze. Hesitantly she glanced at the entrance, images of the redhead bursting through the door made her neck stiff. *Relax, you're safe here.* Taking a deep breath, she focused on the conversation and background music to settle her nerves.

The last of the dinner dishes were taken to the sink. Kelly sat at the table finishing her glass of wine. A loud crack of smashing glass followed by a car alarm disrupted the relaxing music in the lounge room. Brett stuck his head out of the kitchen, "What was that?"

Kelly peered out the front window, "Mum's car!" She ran out onto the footpath. A three-foot steel pole stuck out of the smashed windscreen. *Where did that come from?* She froze her eyes darting around the street. Several cars were parked along the curb with no activity. She pulled out her phone to call the police when something moved behind her. The redhead woman stepped out of the shadows.

"Put away the phone." She slowly stepped closer, "I warned you to stay away from him."

"Brett!" Kelly's scream echoed along the street. Scampering backwards her eyes were fixed on the redhead.

The woman launched herself at Kelly. She dived to the side, landing on the lawn and narrowly avoiding her attacker. She scrambled to get back on her feet. The redhead jumped on her back grabbing a fistful of hair. Breathing heavily, Kelly winced as she reached up pushing her palm into the woman's face. "Get off me," Kelly grunted. Her gaze was drawn over the woman's shoulder as Brett grabbed the stranger around the throat and pulled her back.

Kelly rolled out of the way, gasping for breath as Brett took on the fight. After a short wrestle, the redhead woman was face down with Brett sitting on her back; her arm twisted behind her in an arm lock. "Call the police," he gasped.

"They are on their way," his father replied running down the stairs.

Kelly sat up wiping the blood off her eyebrow. *More blood.* Her eyes looked back at the shattered glass around her mother's car. She closed her eyes and dropped her head as tears ran down her cheek. Taking several deep breaths. *What have I got myself into?*

Brett's mother cautiously approached, handing Kelly some tissues. The wail of a police siren grew louder as the car turned into the street. Kelly looked up as the police car parked in the driveway beside her. One officer secured the redhead while the other interviewed the witnesses; about half the street. Brett held out his hand helping Kelly to her feet. She threw her arms around him, her body trembling.

They stood on the footpath arm in arm staring back at the redhead's face. Kelly took comfort in his embrace as tears rolled down her face. The redhead handcuffed, yelled abuse at them both as the police officer shoved her into the back of the car. All the noise and flashing lights had drawn the attention of the neighbours. Brett panned the growing crowd, "Let's go inside."

A female officer followed them indoors. With the door closed Kelly flopped into the chair dropping her face into her shaking hands. She wiped her cheek with a soggy tissue. Brett returned with some ice wrapped it in a tea towel and placed it on her temple. They explained the problems of the last few days to the police officer.

Kelly holding the ice pack on her head, looked back at Brett when he paused mid-sentence looking blankly at the door. His attention came back to the room as he sat forward on the couch, "I think that maybe Tania Beacham."

"You know her?" Kelly lowered the ice from her aching head.

"Not really, she was expelled from my grade ten class for fighting the other girls."

"Well, she hasn't changed," Brett's mother replied handing Kelly a glass of cold water.

"These girls she used to fight with, did they hang around you?

"I didn't notice."

Kelly got off the phone with her parents and turned towards Brett, "Can you run me home? I can't drive that car."

Cruising down the road, Brett reached out taking hold of her hand, "I was concerned when you didn't come back for your drink. You didn't seem the type to ditch on a date."

"It was hardly a date."

"Let's find somewhere quiet and talk."

"Sounds good. I'll text my parents so they don't worry."

Brett slowed as they approached a roadhouse on the edge of town, "Do you want something to eat or drink?"

"Water will be fine."

After a short cruise down the highway, they turned into an old haunt from school, a lookout on the hill overlooking the town. Kelly sat on the flat rock ledge near the lookout. Below her the dark plain sparkled with the town lights. The quarter moon hung low on the horizon. Everything was dark except for the bright Milky Way stretching out overhead. *This brings back so many memories of my teenage years. Spending our weekends up here with schoolmates partying and staring at the stars. There wasn't much to do here back then. I wonder if Brett was ever up here with them?*

"You know one thing I loved doing out here," she laid back on the rock staring at the sea of stars above.

"Kissing hot guys?"

"The hot ones were taken. We would compete to see who spotted the first satellite or meteorite."

"Yeah, I remember that." The touch of his shoulder against her as he took hold of her hand made her pulse rise.

The night was still, and peaceful, Kelly had a big sigh as her nerves eased, "Thank you for the rescue."

"No problem. She was crazy. This is not how I expected to spend Christmas in a small town," he said. "I think it's safer in Sydney."

What? Her head turned towards him, "Do you live in Sydney?"

"Yep. Seven Hills."

We have been living in the same town all these years. "Small world. I live at Quakers Hill." She rolled towards him, "When are you heading home?"

"The bus leaves on Tuesday."

"We are on the same bus," her mood lifted as she rolled back. *I haven't seen him for over a decade and now he lives next door.*

"Quakers Hill, that's unreal. What job do you have?" He asked.

"Workplace trainer at a corporate management training college. What about you?"

"Franchise manager."

"What does that entail?" Her eyes tracked an airline in the upper atmosphere. The distance blinking lights slowly moving across the sky added to the mesmerising stars.

"I travel around keeping the local franchises profitable."

"Sounds complicated."

"Training super egos sounds just as bad."

The warmth of his body was matched by the heat radiating from the rock ledge in the cool night air. The silence was broken by bugs chirping in the grass nearby. "What happened to your girlfriend you had in high school?"

"I don't know. She went to a university in France and we stopped talking."

"France. Wow." Taking a moment, "Is there anyone else?"

"No. I haven't found the right one."

Taking a deep breath, she paused briefly, "I had a sweet spot for you at school."

"I know. I liked you too." He shuffled beside her, "Looking back I don't know why I was dating that girl."

He knew? What was going on in his head back then?

He rolled over facing Kelly, placing his arm across her stomach, "These last few days have been crazy. When we get home, let's have dinner and start fresh."

A date. He wants to see me again. She reached up in the darkness, the stubble on his jawline was rough under her fingers. Drawing his face closer, "Kiss me," she whispered.

With no reply, the touch of his hand cupping her cheek made her pulse jump. His soft lips were warm against hers.

After a big sleep-in, Kelly sat on the front veranda, sunglasses shading her puffy eyes. She sipped her coffee. *My head, I can't handle wild nights out anymore.* The sound of a motor car came up the driveway, she slowly raised her head. *Mum's car with a windscreen, I am seeing things?*

Brett climbed out of the driver's seat, "All fixed." *A blue office shirt and shorts; that's dressed up for a car delivery.*

"How?"

"I had the windscreen replaced this morning," he replied climbing the stairs.

She rose, greeting him with a welcome hug, "Thanks." He stepped back and held out the keys. "How did you get the keys?"

"I came over earlier and got them off your mother. You were sleeping." He lowered her glasses, "But it looks like you need more."

"I spent the evening with you, there is only one person to blame for this face."

"Tania."

She looked over the glasses still partway down her nose, "Don't remind me." She pushed her glasses up as she returned to her seat and took another mouthful of coffee. "What are you up to today?"

He edged down beside her, he had a nervous jiggle as he ran his palms up his shorts, "I can't wait until we get home for a date. How about a picnic along the river? Unless you have other ideas."

"That sounds good."

He tapped his hand on her thigh, "Get dressed, we have to drop by the police station on the way and finalise our statements."

She groaned as she climbed out of the chair, "Sounds like fun." *A first date at the police station, that's something I want to remember.*

Sign here, here and here the officer flicked through the pages. "Remove your makeup and stand against that screen," the officer handed Kelly a container of sterile wipes.

What the? "Why?"

"Photos for the evidence file."

"You got photos last night."

"That was in the dark. We need pics of any further bruising."

Oh, Great. She winced as the alcohol wipes stung the scratches on her cheek.

She glanced sideways at the computer monitor, her puffy eyes and purple cheekbone stood out. *I could use that for my new profile pic. I think not.* Slipping her sunglasses on as she left the police station, she looked back to Brett, "Ready for lunch with Mike Tyson."

"A few bruises and scratches. It's temporary." He touched the top of her chest, "I'm drawn to what's inside. Looks come and go." Turning along the footpath he reached over and plucked a rose from the police garden and handed it to her.

"Just pinch a rose from the police station."

He opened the car door, "If you don't want it put it back."

Buckled up in the passenger seat, she held up the flower. The red petals had just started to open. She closed her eyes as she took a whiff of the perfume. "Where have you been in my life?"

"Living around the corner so it seems."

She leaned over placing her head on his shoulder, "What are we having for lunch?"

"I don't know I haven't bought it yet."

Reclined on the rug under the gum tree, she overlooked the dry river bed. A ribbon of sand and rocks sprawled out below. Kelly looked up at a squawk above her, a magpie sat on a branch eyeing off her food. *Hello, little fellow. I better hide my lunch.* She tossed a couple of chips over the creek bank. *That has got rid of him for a while.* Swiping a fly off her chicken, she grabbed a chip, "Do you think you will ever move back out here?"

"It's beautiful but there aren't a lot of opportunities out here," he took a mouthful of soft drink.

"Do you ever remember this river flowing?"

"Only after the wet season."

She jumped as a magpie dived down taking her last piece of chicken. Looking up in the tree, two more birds glared back. "I think our secret is out."

"Yeah, let's go."

Christmas is over. Waving goodbye to her parents, Kelly rested at the café, waiting for the bus home. Brett sat beside her, "You made page four," dropping the small local newspaper on the table.

A town this small and I only got on page four. The front page had a big spread on Santa visiting the local daycare centre. She turned to page four; her eyes quickly scanned the page. *Where is it?* She looked closer. *'Tania Beacham was charged with wilful damage and common assault.'* "Is that all?"

"Dad said she was charged with assault about six months ago. She should get longer in jail this time."

The bus pulled up against the curb, Kelly rose and placed her bags beside the cargo hold, "We are not to talk about her again."

A week later, back in Sydney, Kelly's phone rang. *Brett is early tonight.*

"Hey, I have to postpone our date. I have to fly up to Newcastle tomorrow. We are opening a new shop up there and I have to oversee the setup and training."

"When will you be back?"

"I'm away for two weeks.

Two weeks, that's a long time. "Where are you staying?"

"The Sunshine apartments."

The following Friday evening, the flight from Sydney was packed. Kelly exited the terminal and climbed into the taxi, "Sunshine Apartments."

Standing at the entrance she panned the block. *Six storeys of white concrete and glass, how the hell am I going to find him?* Street lamps added a dull glow to the footpath but the neon hamburger sign stood out the most. *Takeaway. I am hungry.*

She placed the bag of food on the reception counter. "Home delivery for Brett Rolland. Fifth floor. The assistant didn't write the room number on the docket."

"Fifth floor. Room eleven."

"Thanks."

Waiting at the lift doors, the numbers counted down. *I can't believe that worked.* Her excitement grew as she made her way along the hallway. She paused before knocking. *I hope he is in.* The door opened, and Brett looked back stunned briefly. His casual shorts and cotton T-shirt said he was in for the night.

"Kelly, what are you doing here?"

"We had a date booked. The place doesn't matter," she held up the bag, "I hope you're hungry."

He smiled and stepped aside, "Come in." Taking the bag from her hand, he leaned over with a kiss.

"How did you find me?"

"You said on the phone last night, you could see the whole beach from the fifth floor." She followed him into the kitchenette, "I gave the receptionist the floor and she gave me your room number."

"Are you sure you're not a detective?"

She stepped forward wrapping her arms around his chest, "No, just someone who wanted to see you."

He looked up at the clock, "Why don't I get changed and we have dinner on the beach."

She sat next to him on a bench overlooking the shoreline. The golden street lights behind her danced with the moonlight on the waves below. A few couples are out walking along the sand. Kelly's long blonde hair fluttered in the warm ocean breeze. Brett ran his fingers over her cheek brushing her hair off her face, "I always liked your hair."

"Your eyes captured me. You can tell so much from someone's eyes."

He placed his arm across her back, "What are my eyes telling you?"

Right now? It's dark. "You have a warmth and passion but you're gentle with the right person."

"With the right person, I am all those things and more."

"I have seen that side," she opened the bag, "Speaking of warmth, better eat dinner before it's cold."

Opening the wrapper, Brett paused, "Does it have pickles?"

"No, I know you don't like them."

"How can you remember that? I can't remember what I did last week," he took a bite of the burger.

Picking up her burger, "Somethings are easy to remember," her voice softened, "You wearing your favourite blue shirt, listening to Phil Collins sitting on the hill near the campfire—". The memory was disrupted when his warm lips met hers. The taste of his bar-b-que sauce lingered on her lips. She slowly unwrapped her burger as she looked out over the waves.

"Where are you staying tonight?" He asked.

"I had my bags delivered to Level Two."

"Why didn't you just stay with me? You didn't need a separate room."

"And what would I do if you weren't here."

He packed up his rubbish, "Well I'm here. Let's have a walk."

The waves lapped the shore as they strolled arm in arm in the moonlight. "I have missed this for the last fifteen years," he said.

"This?"

"Someone to share moments like this with."

"I can't believe you have always been fifteen minutes down the road." Her voice choked on the words. Taking a deep breath, she snuggled her head into his shoulder. "Why haven't we ever met at previous family Christmas parties?"

"My family rotates Christmas each year at a different relative."

"I'm glad our stars aligned this year."

He stopped and turned in front of her, "Let's get your bags from level two and take them to level five."

Kelly was sorting through her luggage when the music playing in the lounge became stereo in the hall. *What the?* She stuck her head out the doorway. A second deep voice resonated from the bathroom. His soulful serenade filled the air. Kelly's eyes widened as she stood with her ear beside the closed door. *He never said he could sing.* Listening to his voice belting out those words, brought a lump to her chest. Closing her eyes she silently mouthed the words as she was taken to another place.

She jumped as the bathroom door opened. Brett stopped singing mid-sentence as he came face-to-face with her. "Do you need the bathroom?

"No," she slowly raised her eyes following the contours of every muscle on his bare torso. Taking a deep breath, her heart skipped a beat. His broad chest muscles stood out above the towel wrapped around his hips. She lightly coughed, "Just listening. I didn't know you could sing."

"More of a casual pastime," he wandered into his bedroom.

"You should do it professionally," she called out from the hall.

"I have an agent. I perform at gigs every now and then."

"Like what?"

"Weddings, musicals, a backup singer and that sort of thing."

"Let me know when you have your next gig. I want to hear more."

She was still outside the bathroom door when he left the bedroom. His eyes connected with hers as he walked past. "There is a name for people who hang out near bathrooms." He laughed as he kept walking.

In the shower, Kelly let the hot water run over her back. Memories of him singing moments ago kept circling in her head. *I don't remember him ever doing music at school.* She wiped her hair as she went to get changed.

He was leaning back in the lounge, sipping a glass of water. A second glass sat on the coffee table. The music still played in the background. As she sat down the song changed, Brett reached over to the remote turning up the volume, "I like this one."

His rich voice blended with the tune like he was in the band. Kelly stared back at every word coming from his lips. He turned towards her, locking eyes as he broke into chorus. A heat rose through her body. Part of her wanted to hear his singing, the other part had other ideas. The longer she sat there the more the second half won the battle. *Oh, what the hell.* She partly rose, throwing her leg over his lap. He was not expecting this reaction, his voice fell silent as his gaze followed her over him. Straddling his thighs she looked down at his soulful eyes, cupping his jaw as she leaned forward with a passionate kiss.

Her fingers ran through his hair; her head arched as his stubble nuzzled her neck. A shiver ran down her spine. His arms embraced her waist; his hands under her shirt slowly climbed her back. With every breath getting heavier, she ripped her shirt off over her head. His lips caressed hers as they fell back on the lounge.

Six months later, it was Friday afternoon, work was over for another week. Kelly unlocked the door, kicking off her shoes as she grabbed her mail from the floor. Brett had been busy with work and preparing for some choir event that was coming up. While tired from a busy week, she looked forward to catching up with him on the weekend.

Flicking through the letters as she headed for the bedroom, a handwritten envelope with *'Important'* on the top line caught her eye. Tearing open the tab she pulled out a concert ticket and a program. 'Choirs of Soul Gala at the Opera House.' She scanned the program. *Numerous choirs.* Her eyes widened at the line, *'Featuring Brett Rolland and Lorna Collins singing, All I Ask of You from Phantom of the Opera!' What? When is this?* Her eyes darted down the page. "Tomorrow night! I have to get a dress."

After trying on numerous dresses in the shop, she looked back at the simple slimline black evening dress. The silky fabric hung down and lightly draped on the floor. It showed elegance but didn't yell 'Look at me.' *This will go well with my jewellery.*

A stranger wearing a suit opened the taxi door at the Opera House. She stepped out straightening her dress. Her long blonde hair was slicked back at the sides with sparkling hair combs. Pulling the shawl over her shoulders she focused on climbing each step in her four-inch heels. Making the walk alone quickened her pace as the crowd closed in at the door.

Standing in the corner waiting for the theatre doors to open, she scanned the foyer. *I won't see him before the show, he will be busy. Wow, some people are dressed up like they are meeting the queen. It's just a choir event.*

Taking a seat, the orchestra warmed up in the background. The lights started to dim, Kelly glanced beside her, the chair was empty.

Did he book that for later? Being so close to the stage in the second row alone gave her butterflies. Her insecurities dropped as the audience fell into darkness.

The fourth choir left the stage and the hall went dark. The crowd fell silent when the haunting boom of the pipe organ overhead blasted out the well-known theme of the Phantom of the Opera. A chill ran over her body. The spotlight rose revealing a fancy-dressed female singer centre stage. As the orchestra took over from the pipe organ Brett slowly stepped into the light. He looked the part in the full-length black suit and classic white phantom mask. Kelly's eyes were fixed on him as he raised his microphone to his lips. She held her breath as a tightness grabbed her chest.

His deep voice filled the hall, each note burnt into her soul. She peered back through the darkness as goosebumps rose over her body. The crowd melted away as they were the only two people in the room. He turned looking directly back at her, his arm outstretched towards her as his voice roared out the chorus. Her heart skipped a beat as every nerve in her body trembled. She was being drawn into his world.

He turned back to the female singer and continued. Kelly's eyes filled with tears as her emotions took over. His booming voice echoed inside her. And as the last note faded the stage went black. The audience rose to their feet clapping. Slowly the walkway lights came on as the interval buzzer rang out. Kelly sat for a moment taking a deep breath. She stared back at the stage, trying to regain her composure.

Interval, Kelly checked her makeup in the powder room before joining the others in the foyer. A passing waiter handed her a glass of champagne. Raising the glass to her lips, she panned the room when a side door opened. The crowd stood aside as her eye caught a tall figure across the room. He wore the same black suit and the white mask, holding a single long-stemmed red rose. His eyes fixed on her as he headed straight toward her. Each stride with purpose and without question. Her chest tightened and her cheeks flushed. Inside she wanted to disappear as the crowd turned towards her. Some of the crowd held up their phones taking pictures. Her stomach twisted in knots as her palms became sweaty. *What are you doing Brett?* The glass in her hand started to shake, she slipped it on the side table.

In that costume, he exuded a power, a confidence she had not seen before. He stood before her not saying anything as he handed her the rose. Taking the flower, she smiled to hide her nerves. His eyes locked on hers as he dropped to one knee. The foyer lit up with camera flashes as he held out his hand. "Kelly Spanning, will you marry me."

Her eyes dropped to his hand, an open box with a diamond solitaire ring stared back at her. The tears returned as she reached for his hands. "Yes."

Taking hold of her hand he slipped the diamond on her finger. He rose wrapping his arms around her and leaned in for a kiss. She looked back at the mask, tilting her head more than normal before her lips met his. The camera flashes continued as the clapping got louder. She took hold of his arm as he returned to the stage door. The walk took longer than it should as people wanted photos of him in character arm in arm with his new fiancé. Time was running in slow motion as she looked back at his face partly covered in the mask. On the arm of a celebrity character in a social media storm. *Have I fallen into a fantasy story?*

The stage door closed behind them. Kelly took a deep breath, burying her face in her hands as she dropped her forehead on his chest. Her body trembled as tears rolled down her cheeks. He wrapped his arms around her in a reassuring embrace. "Are you all right?" His soft tender voice had returned.

"Yes," she stepped back and blotted her tears on a tissue. The interval buzzer rang. He reached out for another hug, "Take that mask off if you want a kiss."

With the swipe of his hand, the mask was gone. He leaned in with another passionate kiss. "Do you want to see the rest of the show?"

Her shoulders dropped, "I don't know how much more I can take tonight."

"I have finished singing for the night; we can go home."

The foyer was a lot quieter as they left. Climbing into the taxi the overhead high reflected off the rock on her finger. Sitting quietly on the way home, she outstretched her hand staring at the ring. *What happened tonight?*

He reached over placing his hand on her forearm, "Did you enjoy tonight?"

"It hasn't sunk in yet," she dropped her head on his shoulder, "It still feels like a dream."

He slid his arm behind her back, hand on her shoulder as he drew her closer. "You looked stunning tonight," he whispered.

The following morning, Brett placed the breakfast tray on her bedside table. "Morning dear." Taking a sip of coffee, he placed the folded newspaper on her lap. "We made page two."

Page two! She held up the paper. A quarter-page picture of the Phantom of the Opera on a knee with her standing over him trying to hold it together. *'After performing on stage, local Tenor Brett Rolland proposed to Kelly Spanning at last night's gala show.'*

She leaned over with a kiss, "The night was perfect but if you do that again, I will kill you."

"I could have serenaded you first. But I thought that was a bit much," he sat beside her, "I'll leave that for the wedding."

She glanced sideways, "As long as you are the only one doing the serenading. No duets."

"I chose that song for you," he reached out for a hug.

She snuggled into his warm embrace; her eyes drawn to the photo in the paper. "Did you get copies for our folks?"

"Done." He said, "And I'm getting the pictures from the choir members."

"How many knew you were planning this?"

"The whole choir and gala management," he replied with a smile.

Everyone. Her phone buzzed; she glanced at the screen, "Facebook?" Looking back at the video of the phantom proposing to her felt like an out-of-body experience. Followed by a few photos on the choir's page with hundreds of likes. She lowered her phone, "I'm not going to hear the end of this."

He took hold of her phone and placed it on the side table. She laid back as he leaned over her, "The night was special to me and I hope it was for you too."

"I will never forget it."

The End.The End of Story 1.

SHORT STORY 2

TWO RED ROSES

Contemporary Christmas Romance
Sequel to Single Red Rose

Written By C. L. Hamilton

C. L. Hamilton

2. TWO RED ROSES

It's been a month since that night at the Sydney Opera House. I can never forget how he asked me to marry him. How he set up his choir and the gala managers to allow him to sing 'All I Ask of You from the Phantom of the Opera.' It was a duet with another female choir member but the song was aimed at me. His loving eyes stared back at me in the darkness, he knew exactly where I was sitting. He went full in with the full-length suit and the famous white mask partly hiding his face. His rich tenor voice reverberated around the hall. I'm shaking just thinking about it now.

The first time I heard him sing I was in the motel hall; he was in the shower pumping out a serenade to the music playing in the lounge. I was amazed then but his Phantom of the Opera performance blew me away. I hadn't recovered from his performance when he approached me in the foyer minutes later still in costume with a single red rose and a ring. His proposal made page two of the daily paper. Sydney a city of five million was not big enough to hide in after that. I can't even hide back home as Mum would have told everyone several times over by now.

And in case I should ever forget, he has a four-foot-high print of him in full Phantom costume on his knee proposing to me in front of the whole foyer. The print is on the main display in the lounge room for anyone entering the front door to see. He seems very proud of his achievements that night. I'm proud of him too. When I went home for Christmas last year this was not where I expected to end up. And now that the news of our engagement is out, we are heading home to visit our parents who keep harassing us with questions.

A thud came from the front door, "Brett is that you?"

"Yeah, the bus leaves in an hour are you ready?" He walked into the bedroom, wrapping his arms around her waist. "Hi darling," leaning forward with a smile and a sweet kiss.

Even dressed casually, he still looked dashing in the blue shirt and denim shorts. That shade of blue brought out his warm hazel eyes. She smiled as she grabbed her phone charger from the bedside table and tossed it in her handbag.

Brett clutched her suitcase as they headed for the elevator. "I have booked the motel."

Relaxing on the bus, Kelly looked back over her shoulder. The last of Sydney's skyline dropped below the tree line. She turned back to Brett taking his hand, "This feels very different to the last time I was heading home on this bus."

"You're not alone this time."

"Are your folks harassing you to stay with them?" She asked.

"Yeah, but there is no room for both of us."

"Same, my mother wants to put a swag on the floor for you."

"A swag? I think we will stick with the motel."

Kelly leaned her head on the window, gazing at the passing landscape. *The same hills and rivers. A few new housing estates are in the process of construction.* A water bottle appeared in front of her. Looking back at Brett as she smiled taking the bottle.

"What are you thinking?" He asked.

"Our parents are pestering us about where to stay this week. How are we going to plan this wedding with them butting in?"

"It's our wedding. We can assign them some jobs and we organise the rest," he leaned in closer his face inches away, his eyes connecting with hers. "Don't worry." She closed her eyes as his lips met hers.

Brett's parent's house hasn't changed. She stepped out of her mother's car; nervously scanning the street. Turning to Brett, "The last time I was here—"

"That lunatic smashed up my car," Kelly's mother added as she walked past them both.

Thanks, Mum. Kelly dropped her head, as her shoulders sank.

Brett stepped toward her, cupping her jaw with his palms, "Look at me. That was a long time ago. I'm here now."

"It's OK, she got locked up and her bail was refused," Kelly's father muttered casually as he walked up the path. Kelly grabbed a quick hug from Brett. "Are you two coming?" Her father called out from the front door.

"Parents," Kelly murmured as they made their way up the path arm-in-arm. Brett had her under one arm and a large carry bag in the other. "What's in the bag? She asked.

"Just stuff mum wanted."

Everyone sat around the dining table with a beer in hand. Both sets of parents were constantly talking and asking questions. Before anyone could answer another question had been thrown into the ring. Brett reached into his bag and pulled out the photos of the engagement proposal he had received from the gala guests.

His father looked over the pictures as they were handed around the table. "And what would you have done if she had said no?"

"You weren't there. I put a lot of preparation into making sure she said yes." Pulling out his laptop, he brought up the stage performance and the proposal videos.

That haunting sound of his voice pierced my soul. I was back in the audience that night staring back at his eyes with the same wave of emotion rising inside me. She wiped her cheek. *Am I ever going to stop crying when I hear his singing?* She looked up as the video ended, and both mothers had tears running down their cheeks. *So, it's not just me.*

"Well done. With that performance, someone else would have jumped forward if she had said no."

Kelly sat bolt upright in her seat, "Dad, you can't say that."

"I would have said yes," Kelly's mother mumbled. Kelly raised her eyes towards her mother and then back at Brett without saying anything.

"So, why the visit?" Brett's father asked.

"Just some family time before we all meet for the wedding."

The chatter went on. Questions were being asked about topics that hadn't been worked out yet. The early start, the bus trip and the talking were draining. "We need to check into the motel and have a break," Kelly rose from the table.

Back in the motel room Brett reached into his bag and pulled out a white folder placing it in front of Kelly. The words Wedding Planner stood out on the cover.

"What's this?" Kelly looked back confused.

"A gift from someone I used to work with in town. I didn't pull it out at the house as it would have started our first family fight."

Kelly was flicking through the pages. "You have written 'Brett to plan' in the music section."

"Yeah, I will look after all that."

"Don't I get a say?"

"We can't do it all, you focus on the bridal party and decorations. I will focus on the music and the groom stuff."

"What's your plan? An orchestra led by Andrew Lloyd Webber?"

"No, he has retired."

"And if he wasn't?" She snapped back.

He dropped down beside her on the bed, placing his hands on her shoulders, "Trust me. Did I stuff up the proposal?"

"No," she sighed and dropped her eyes as they filled with tears, "But I'm scared you'll do something beautiful and I will fall apart in front of everyone again."

He wrapped his arms around her in a firm embrace. "You can do this— we can do this." Sitting upright, he wiped her cheek with his thumb. "I know a wedding planner who calls me when someone rich wants a wedding singer. She told me you can discuss anything with her," he tapped her shoulder as he rose, "When we get home, call her." He looked back from the doorway, "Grab your jacket, we are going for a drive."

"Where?"

"Our old haunt, we'll get some dinner on the way."

"Don't we have dinner at your folks tonight?" She asked climbing into the car they had borrowed from her mother.

"I told them we had other plans. We will catch up with them tomorrow."

Back on their familiar hilltop, she sat down on the rock ledge near the town lookout. The sun slowly melted into the horizon; the dust lingering in the air created a blood-red cloudless sky. As the darkness crept in, the town below slowly lit up. Brett sat beside her, watching the sunset as they ate their fish and chips.

The last rays of the sun disappeared, and the cold night air blew in. "Shame there is a fire ban. I could go with a campfire now," she moved closer and placed her head on his shoulder. "Feels like I'm seventeen again, hiding away from my parents and chilling."

"The company is better this time," he reached for his phone, "I know what we are missing." He flicked through his phone tuning on some relaxing music.

A Phil Collins song played and Brett started to sing along. "Stop that. I'm not crying tonight."

"Sing it with me."

"I never took singing lessons." She said, "And when did you find out you could sing?"

"In my twenties, I was singing along to some music at home. My flatmate was in the choir and dragged me to a practice session."

She took hold of his arm, "Your voice is stunning, you could make a living out of it."

"My agent has been bugging me to do more after the phantom video went viral."

"Why are you holding back?"

"I don't have time with work."

"Change jobs. You can do it."

"Let's deal with the wedding first." He laid back on the rock ledge, "Lay down, I brought you up here to chill."

The Milky Way sprayed across the sky. With no moon, each star was brighter than usual. She laid back, taking hold of his hand she silently let the stress drift away. "Do you remember what I said last Christmas when we were up here?"

"There was a lot said."

She leaned over him, "Kiss me."

Back in Sydney, still recovering from her family visit, Kelly stood on a box looking back at the mirror. The white satin gown fitted snugly around her waist and then softly fell to the floor. Floral lace ran up her arms meeting each side of her cleavage. The deep drop at the back of the gown made it easier to get in and out of. Random pearl drops accented the rose lace.

"What are your plans for the veil?" The dressmaker asked as she adjusted the waistline.

"I'm not having one. I want a floral piece and white ribbon in some fancy hairstyle.

Chilling after a day at the dressmaker, Kelly sat on her bed and sipped coffee. Her eyes burned as she stared at the blank pages. *Flowers, gifts, guest list, catering, venue details, cars, nuts or chocolates. I can't do this.* "Argh!" Kelly slammed the wedding plan closed and tossed it across the bed. *It's been a month and pages are still bare.*

Brett pulled his head from the wardrobe, "Are you OK?"

"So much crap to do."

"I will call Beverly, the wedding planner I told you about." He threw his socks into his overnight bag, "I have to dart up to Newcastle for the night, the manager is having problems. We don't have time to plan the whole wedding. Time to delegate."

"Take me with you," she rose from the bed, standing before him.

"Nice thought but the flight is booked out," with a kiss and a hug, "Watch a movie, have a bath, chill. We will worry about the wedding when I get back tomorrow."

A few days later, Kelly had the morning off and was booked to meet Brett in town, he won't say why. She walked the street searching for a shop number. Stopping out of front of the address she scanned the building. *A sound studio? Why does he want to meet me here?*

Approaching the receptionist she was greeted with a smile, "He is in the room on the left."

She didn't ask who I was. Another person who remembers me from the newspaper? Kelly returned a smile as she entered the room. Brett was sitting with another gentleman both with earphones on.

"Hi dear, here put these on," he handed her a set of earphones.

I was thrown back to the Opera House as Brett's rich tenor voice roared over the orchestra playing in the background. When did he have time to do this?

The song ended as the music faded. Brett pulled off his earphones, and his face lit up with excitement, "What do you think."

Kelly fought back the tears, "Beautiful. What's this for?"

"My debut album. It goes on sale just before Christmas."

Her eyes widened, "Album. Wow, you did it." Lunging forward with a warm hug.

"I'm giving a copy to each of the wedding party. As a thank you."

She looked down at the list of songs, 'Nothing Is Going to Change My Love for You,' 'All I Ask of You,' 'Waiting for a Girl Like You,' 'In Case You Didn't Know,' 'Lady Lady Lady.' The list went on and the tear she was fighting off escaped followed by some more. "How the hell am I going to able to listen to this without bursting into tears?"

"I will just have to condition you with more singing."

"You will have to get used to it when it hits the radio," the sound technician added.

Radio, oh crap. He will be everywhere. Her alarm buzzed; she leaned towards Brett, "Are you finished, we have dance lessons in an hour."

Arriving at the studio, Brett loaded the music file. Kelly looked down at the display screen. "Andre Rieu Ballade Pour Adeline. At least you can't sing to that."

We went with a simple waltz; we didn't have time to learn a whole stage production. The dance didn't take long to learn. It was more like clearing the cobwebs from dance classes at school.

Kelly sat at the table blankly staring at her laptop. The wedding was two weeks away. With her full-time job and the wedding stress, she had shut down. Brett organised Deb and Sal her old school friends and bridesmaids to come down and pull her back together. The first task on the list was the final fitting of the bridal outfits. The bridesmaid's dresses and accessories were Brett's favourite colour, Cobalt Blue. Kelly looked back at Deb in her dress; the blue was a pure colour that sat perfectly with the white roses.

Five days to go. Kelly sat at her work desk and pulled another file from the tray. *Both sets of parents have arrived in town, they are staying in a motel. One advantage of living in an one bedroom apartment. I get some peace after hours. The wedding planner has arranged for everyone to meet at the function centre this evening to revise the final plan. Today is my last day at work for three weeks. I will have to audit this paperwork when I return as very little of it is registering in my fried brain.*

Entering the hall, the emergency exit was the only thing visible in the darkness. A flick of the switch brought it to life. *Wow, it's big.* The floor was lined with tables, a bar in one corner and a small stage in the other. Kelly and Brett wandered around looking at the table layout plan. The noise level increased when their parents and bridesmaids arrived. Brett was leaning on the bar discussing the drinks menu when Sal and Deb bounced up behind him, "Vodka on the rocks please."

Two more people arrived, Kelly froze mid-sentence, "No bloody way."

"What's the problem?" Brett glanced in the direction of Kelly's gaze.

The wedding planner was at the door with the photographer she had hired. A big head of red hair glowed under the entry lights. She was about the same size as Tania the woman who attacked Kelly at Christmas back home.

Kelly turned away. Images of that red-haired psycho hitting her in the toilet filled her thoughts. Her chest tightened as the same urgency to escape returned. She grabbed her bag and took off for the back door.

"Where are you going?" Sal called out.

Kelly was partway across the back carpark when Deb and Sal caught up with her. Focused on the gardens ahead, Kelly kept walking. With no street lamps, the park was a mix of moonlight and long shadows.

"Kelly, stop." Deb grabbed her arm.

Kelly pulled away, "Did you see who was with the planner?"

"She is just a photographer—"

Brett bolted around the corner, pulling up in front of Kelly. "What has happened?"

"We need a different photographer."

He paused briefly, "It's not Tania, she is in jail."

"I'm stressed enough, I don't need to be reminded of that crazy cow every time I look up!" Her voice went horse as she held back her rant.

"Where are we going to find another photographer now?"

"I don't care! Get one of the guests to do it." Kelly snapped back, as she stormed off further into the garden. It didn't take long for Brett to catch up with her.

Surrounded by bushes and darkness, Brett took hold of her hand, "We need a photographer," his voice softened.

She whipped her arm back, "Everyone keeps saying it's my day. Well, I'm the only one who doesn't get a say in any of it!" Waving her hands around her voice rose as she let go, "Mum is bossing the caterer around, Deb and Sal are doing their own thing, and you won't tell me what you're planning." She gasped. "The wedding planner is working off a list created by everyone else. The only thing I have had any say in is my dress." She turned her back to him dropping her head into her hands.

"It's stressful, I know."

She took a deep breath as she spun around. "Why am I here? They probably haven't even noticed I'm gone!" Tears rolled down her cheeks.

He stepped forward, taking hold of her hands, "We don't have to do this tonight. We can see the planner tomorrow morning. Just the two of us."

She dropped her head onto his shoulder, "That would be good."

"Go wait in the car, I'll deal with the others," he pulled the keys from his pocket handing them to her.

"I want to talk when we get home, just you and me. No one else."

"Won't be long." He leaned in with a soft kiss before heading off to the hall.

Her eyes followed him as he moved from the moonlight into the shadows. *Peace at last.* She sighed as she stood alone in the darkness. *If I go out the front now, they will catch me as they leave.* Strolling back through the garden she rested on a bench seat under the shadow of a tree and in sight of the carpark.

Sitting silently in the dark, she stared back as the vehicles drove off one by one. Brett came out standing beside his car and scanned the area. He headed towards her as she rose from the bench. Meeting part way they returned silently arm in arm.

She looked back from the passenger seat on the way home, Brett went to ask her something. She turned the music up loud and turned to look out the window. He reached out touching her thigh. She briefly glanced back as a tear trickled down her cheek. No words were spoken on the trip home.

The front door closed Brett turned the kettle on as Kelly dropped into the lounge pulling her shoes off. Flicking on some relaxing music he handed her a cup, "Camomile Tea." He sat down, turned to face her, and tenderly asked, "What do you want to talk about."

"I want to know all your plans for the reception," she sipped her tea.

"It's nothing to worry about. I have hired a DJ and I'm singing a song for us." He shuffled in the seat as he moved closer. "I told you after our engagement that I would sing at our wedding."

"Is that all?"

"Yes," he paused, "Andrew Lloyd Webber wasn't available," he returned a cheeky grin.

Ha, funny. Taking a mouthful of tea, she placed the cup on the coffee table, "Thanks, I'm going for a shower."

The hot water rained down over her body, she dipped her head forward letting her aching shoulders soak up the heat. Her long hair hung over her face but she didn't care. The shower screen quietly opened. Her senses were heightened as his bare skin touched hers. Brett lightly pushed her hair aside as his lips touched her shoulder. He slid his hands around her waist drawing her closer to his body. She tilted her head, as goosebumps rose over her skin. Her pulse raced with each deep breath. She turned to face him, and slid her arms over his shoulders, drawing him in as her lips caressed his. The cold tiles against her back added to the invigorating sensation.

She winced as the alarm rang out. *My head.* Brett's warm body was nestled against her back, his hand resting on her hips, he leaned over kissing her cheek, "Good morning darling."

"Good morning," she groaned.

"You look tired. How can I help?"

"Coffee," she sat up, "And a shower—I can do that one myself."

"That would be best, we have the planner meeting in an hour."

The peak hour street traffic had waned as the wedding planner arrived. Kelly adjusted her sunglasses. *Why did he choose an outdoor café?* Brett sat beside her, his arm behind her back. The wedding planner leaned over the table working through the plan, noting the amendments and task allocation.

A middle-aged man dropped down beside Brett, "Sorry, I'm late."

What the? Kelly glanced towards them both.

"This is Andrew. He's in my choir. I called him late last night."

"Why?" Kelly whispered.

"Andy is our show photographer. He took the photos of our engagement, including the one on our wall."

With the plan complete, the wedding planner closed the folder, "If you go ahead with cancelling the photographer she will be billing you for the five-hundred-dollar cancellation fee."

"That's fine," Kelly replied.

"I'll email you the revised plan when I get back to the office," the planner packed her bag.

Day zero. Kelly closed her eyes and held her breath as a cloud of hairspray filled the air. Deb handed her a glass of champagne as the makeup artist sorted through her colours. *The wine will only briefly take the nerves off the day. I sent my mother to annoy the wedding planner. Dad is with the groomsmen doing what blokes do before these events. Brett's mother is helping set up the hall.*

Deb and Sal were joined by Brett's brothers' wives making the bridal party of four bridesmaids. They all look smashing in their blue dresses sorting out the flowers. Kelly looked back at the mirror as Sal zipped up the wedding dress. On her third attempt to pick up an earring, Kelly turned to Sal, "Can you put my earrings in? Why did they have to make my fake nails so long?" *I should cut them back.*

"The cars are here," Deb called out.

The limo pulled up in front of one of the bigger churches in town. People lined the footpath. *Aren't they inside yet? Should we wait?* The car door was opened and everyone started climbing out. *Nope, we are going ahead.* She paused on the path, her eyes scanning the crowd as Sal adjusted everything. Her father stood waiting outside the door. Taking her father's arm the pipe organ started followed by a chorus of choir singers. *Of course, he included the choir.* One step at a time she made her way along the aisle. Her heart thumped in her chest. *The church is packed. I don't know most of these people.* The camera flashes brought back memories of the engagement when she could hardly see anything in front of her. She raised her eyes slowly meeting Brett's at the altar. *Breathe, just keep breathing.*

The touch of his hand and his warm eyes kept me grounded in my body. My eyes didn't travel any further for fear of losing control. There was a point when my heart was skipping and I must have looked pale or something. Brett looked back, squeezed my hand and mouthed the words, 'I love you.' A warmth rose inside as I smiled and squeezed his hand back.

A load was lifted off my shoulders when I heard the words, "You may kiss the bride." His kiss was sweet. Like my engagement, most of the ceremony was a blur of fantasy and nerves.

It was over, time to leave. The choir filled the church with song. Kelly took Brett's arm; they made their way down the aisle to more blinding camera flashes. Everyone piled into the limos as the photos were being held in the gardens behind the function hall.

The numerous flowering shrubs created a lovely background to the photos. Brett scanned the horizon. "We have to move to the Rotunda."

There was a bit of stage show set up but it was all planned around getting a photo of us in the rotunda with the sun setting behind us. Maybe we should become wedding planners, he's doing a great job so far.

With the photos finished, Brett and Kelly returned to a nearby motel to change. Arriving at the door, Brett grabbed her arm, "One minute." After unlocking the door, he looked back with a big smile. Sliding his arm behind her back and the other under her thighs he swept her up in his arms carrying her into the room. "Tradition."

Back on her feet, she took a deep breath and enjoyed a cold glass of water. Brett paused before her, pushing a few stray hairs behind her ear, "How are you doing?"

"I'm getting there. I need a massage."

"Ask me later."

She gently placed her arms around him, "The choir was a nice touch."

"Told you I wouldn't stuff it up," his voice softened as he drew his fingers along her jaw, his warm lips meeting hers.

He glanced at the clock, sliding his arm behind her back, "We have an hour before we have to leave," he murmured as he unzipped her gown. Slowly tracing his finger along her collar bone pushing her sleeve down her arm. His warm lips tickled her shoulder. She closed her eyes as his lips crept up her neck. Taking a deep breath, she ran her hands over his shoulders towards his chest. Her fingers unbuttoned his shirt as her lips caressed his. As her dress fell to the floor, he swept off her feet once more.

Kelly held up her makeup mirror checking that she was presentable after their break at the motel. The evening dress she was now wearing didn't cling to her ribs like the wedding gown. Brett ditched the suit and tie for a shirt and slacks. She stepped out of the limo taking Brett's arm as they headed for the reception hall. A group of guests were already at the bar. Approaching the bridal table her eyes widened, "You didn't."

A white Phantom of the Opera mask partly covered two red roses at the front of their table. The brilliant red petals stood out against the blue and white decorations on the table.

"They are just decoration. Keeping the theme going, I added another rose for our partnership."

She leaned towards him, "For a country boy, you are a true romantic."

"Just had to find the right person."

The dinner was all but over, the MC stepped up to the microphone on the stage, "Ladies and Gentlemen, I call Brett and Kelly to the stage."

Brett held out his hand. She whispered in his ear, "I haven't had enough to drink for this."

"You will be all right," he murmured as he guided her to the stage. Checking that the microphone was on, he took hold of her hand and nodded towards the DJ. The slow piano music went for a minute before he raised the microphone to his lips, "The first time—ever I saw your face." His soulful voice sent chills down her back. Tears welled in her eyes. *I knew he was planning a serenade but I couldn't prepare for something so emotionally raw. His voice resonated inside me lifting me off my feet. Squeezing his hand tighter did little to help me from losing it.*

The quests sat in stunned silence as he belted out the chorus. His voice surrounded her as she raised her hand over her face. Tears ran down her cheeks. He stepped closer sliding his arm behind her back and pulling her next to him as he continued singing. Her eyes connected with his. The truth was too much for him as his eyes sparkled with tears.

He finished the last words as the music faded. Everyone erupted with cheers and clapping. Kelly threw her arms around him burying her face in his shoulder. He wrapped his arms around her kissing her cheek.

The MC approached the microphone, "Are we having the bridal dance or some more speeches?"

Kelly was still in his arms her hands trembling, Brett turned to the MC, "I think speeches would be best."

Sal handed Kelly a glass of champagne as she sat down. It was emptied in one mouthful; Sal filled the glass again. Kelly blotted her face with a tissue.

Brett's oldest brother and best man came to the stage, "Brett has always had hidden talents. As a teenager, he was just another geek spending his life studying while the hot guys were out dating but then his hormones kicked in and this is where he ended up." He nodded to someone at the back of the room. A projector lit up casting the Phantom of the Opera performance larger than life on the wall.

Kelly's eyes were fixed on the wall until Brett started singing beside her. He took hold of her hand, his eyes fixed on hers as he repeated his lines. *He couldn't help himself. I bet he planned this with his brother.* Her heart pounded as she was drawn into his eyes. *There was no crying, it could be the extra champagne or I was all cried out from his earlier performance. It could be a mix of both.* After the stage video, the best man added, "That song led to this moments later." The engagement video lit up the wall. Brett was quiet for this one, his focus on the wall. The power and confidence he showed walking through the foyer getting down on one knee still in costume. When the video got to her answer, he reached out pulling her closer with a loving kiss. The guests cheered at the end.

"Are you ready for a dance?" Brett whispered.

She nodded taking his hand as they rose. The MC jumped up; time for the bride and groom to take the floor. With the formal bit done the rest of the night was spent dancing and drinking. The stressful bit was over. Dancing around, Brett broke into song which gave others the courage to join in. The choir quests tunes made up for the family members who were not at the same level.

Moving to the music, I enjoyed myself, looking back at the man I love. I spun around to find his brother in front of me and Brett had moved to the next person in line. Moments later the line changed again. It was only now I realised I didn't really know his brothers at all. They were always in another town at the end of the phone. Oh well, I have the rest of my life to get to know them.

Chilling back home, the wedding photos hang on the wall beside the engagement print. I may not have remembered most of the church service but that didn't matter. Brett had video cameras at the front and back of the church. We have our own movie of the ceremony and the reception.

On the music front, Brett is up to his fourth album. Attending events alone at the Opera House never gets easier. Sitting in the darkness watching him bellow out a song to tug at my heartstrings always brought a tear to my eye. Standing in the foyer at intervals keeps bringing back the ghostly images of Brett dressed as the Phantom of the Opera walking towards me when he proposed. He may have quit his job as a Franchise Manager but he is still travelling around backing up at concerts and singing at a wide range of events. I have moved from full-time trainer to the occasional contract job as I'm often out of town. Brett has been supporting my singing lessons. He has a dream of us both on stage singing duets. When we practice duets, I am less likely to cry as all my focus is on getting it right. I have a way to go, I can't see myself ever topping him when it comes to singing. For now, I will be the chick in a fancy dress on my loving husband's arm at public events.

The End of Story 2.

SHORT STORY 3

RESCUED BY LOVE

A Christmas Firefighter Romance

Written By C. L. Hamilton

3. RESCUED BY LOVE

The landscape was littered with burnt-out cars twisted together. One wreck lay on its side leaning against what was left of a building. Steel drums smouldered; the smoke turned the midday sun a deep shade of orange. Rhea sat high on a platform overlooking the action unfolding below. Sweat trickled down from under her helmet and over her cheek. With a clipboard in her lap, she kept her eye on the stopwatch. The hour ticked over, she held the microphone near her lips, "All Teams go."

The approaching fire truck's sirens drowned out the yells and screams of the casualties hidden in the carnage. The latest fire trainees were busy working their way through the scenario. Firefighters pulled hoses and extinguishers from one truck while others worked on rescuing the casualties. Rhea kept an eye on the clock as the deadline approached. A crew was cutting into the final car when the siren blasted. *That forty-five minutes went quickly.* The practical assessment was over and the crews started reconditioning their equipment. Now the hard part started for the Captain of Training, Rhea Dempsy.

Rhea gathered the academy instructors in the training room to discuss the outcome of the exercise. They were joined by Morgan Searle the local Brigade Captain. He often helped with the practical activities. Numerous student files were passed around the table, each

...

needing written feedback. This was the last stage of the year's training for the latest batch of trainee firefighters.

One trainer got annoyed with the discussion, claiming the class couldn't pass the assessment as they didn't rescue the last two casualties. Rhea glared back clenching her jaw. *It has always got to be him that starts the arguments.* "Rex! You know as well as anyone. This exercise was designed to test the processes, procedures, and an understanding of the last five months of training."

"But they didn't finish!" Rex raised his voice to drown out the others.

Morgan stood up leaning forward over the table, "Calm down everyone. I would be happy if all my rescues only took forty-five minutes." His voice dropped, "I want to finish this meeting before Christmas."

The decades of experience in the room always led to a few battles with the odd ego but a result was reached at the end of the day. With the assessments completed, the trainers left the room. Rhea, dropped her head onto the table, taking a deep breath as she sat up. *If I were the boss, Rex would be gone. It's not like he does a lot around here.*

Morgan patted Rhea on the back, "Great exercise. It kept them busy. I had to hold myself back from jumping into the action."

"You wouldn't have passed," Rhea laughed not looking up from the page as she continued scribbling her signature on another form.

"I'd beat you."

"Like to see you try." She closed the file and dropped it in the box, "Last one, done. Holidays here we come."

"Don't get too excited. We have the awards and Christmas Party tonight," Morgan grabbed the box and headed for the door.

"Do you have your Secret Santa yet?"

"Yep," he replied with a smile placing the box on her desk.

A mumbling din filled the hall as the fire brigades and academy staff came together for a fun night. The overhead lights dimmed letting the fake candles set the festive mood. A random firefighter dressed in an oversized suit played Santa Claus. His goal for the evening was to hand out the Secret Santa presents to the person on the gift tag. He walked up to the table, "Rhea," holding out a one-foot square parcel. It was thin with a ridge on one end. A round spring bounced back under her fingers. *A calendar?* She peeled back a section of paper. A bare-chested male wearing a fire helmet stared back at her through the opening. *They gave me the half-naked Firefighters calendar for next year! What the?*

Gail, one of the office workers, peered over Rhea's arm, "What did you get?"

"The fundraising calendar," she mumbled.

"Cool, open it."

"Why? You've seen it before. You have a box of them on your desk."

"What's wrong with another look?"

"I have trained most of them over the years. It feels weird perving on my students," she whispered not wanting to draw attention.

"Someone must think you need some prompting to find a boyfriend." Gail rose from her seat, "I'm getting another drink, do you want one?"

"Yes, thanks," Rhea grabbed her present off the table and went to shove it in her bag when a white piece of paper slid across the opening. *What is that?* Reaching under the table she peeled the wrapping paper back further and pulled out a folded note. Her eyes widened when she read the words, 'Confidential' scribbled on the back of the folded paper. *What is going on here?* She glanced around the room, as she slipped the note in her purse.

Gail returned with the drinks. Rhea grabbed her purse, "Good timing. I need to go to the girl's room."

Locked in the privacy of the toilet cubicle she opened the note. The handwriting had been written in haste across the page. *'Rhea, you look stunning in that red dress. It reinforces my feelings for you. Love always, Your Secret Santa xx.'*

Her heart skipped a beat as she took a deep breath. *What?* She read it a second time. *Red dress. They are here tonight.* Her palms started to sweat. *I have a one in seventy chance of working out who wrote this.* She thought back to the present it came in. *This note with that calendar. Is that romantic or the start of something creepy? Why expose your feelings and then make the message anonymous?* Her nerves grew at the thought of the room full of firefighters. She sat staring at the writing trying to remember who wrote like that.

"Rhea, they are starting the awards. You are needed on stage," Gail called out from the other side of the cubicle door.

Hurrying back to the table, Rhea slipped her purse into the bag. Her eyes scanned the room. *How the hell am I meant to work this out?*

The Master of Ceremonies (MC) called Rhea and Morgan to the stage to announce the training awards for the year. Lifting her dress hem off the floor, she focused on navigating the stage stairs in her high-heeled shoes. Morgan met her at the top step holding out his hand for support. *He looks handsome in his uniform, the blue evening jacket with epaulettes and all the bling.*

After they had given out their awards Rhea went to step off the stage when Morgan leaned closer to the microphone. "The Regional Commanders Award goes to Training Captain Rhea Dempsy." The room erupted with cheers and wolf whistles.

She stopped dead, her cheeks took on the colour of her red dress. Smiling as she turned around to accept the award. *What else is going to happen tonight?* After a few photos of her holding the shield, she hastened to get off the stage without tripping down the stairs.

Dropping down in her seat, she sculled her glass of wine. "I need another one of those. Make it a bottle." She muttered.

"Congratulations, it's been a big night for you," Gail grabbed Rhea's award taking a closer look.

Rhea turned to stand up, "You don't know the half of it."

A couple of glasses of white wine had settled her nerves. The MC said, "That's the official night over. Time to dance." The music volume increased as people headed for the dance floor.

Rhea walked over to Morgan holding out her hand. His grip was gentle as they weaved among the tables. He slid his arm around her waist she placed her hand on his shoulder and they moved to the music. "I didn't know you could dance," he smiled as they shuffled across the floor.

"I'm rusty, but I feel safer with you than being dragged around by some butt-grabbing bloke."

He pulled his head back, his eyes connecting with hers, "I'm glad you don't include me in that group." Pulling her body closer, he went back to dancing. Spinning around he leaned towards her ear and whispered, "Unless you want me to."

Her eyes briefly connected with his, and she kept dancing without saying a word.

Two days later, the local firehouse received an emergency call. A delivery van had hit a car at the main intersection in town. This was the second accident of the day. Morgan was in his office, preparing for the Christmas holidays when his phone rang.

It was Jeff the Senior Leader of the Fire Unit attending the accident. "Morgan, the driver of the car in this accident is Rhea. The ambulance is treating her now."

Rhea! Morgan jumped in his seat, "Is she OK?" A sharp pain stabbed his chest.

"She's alive and barely conscious. Her car was side-impacted when the van ran a stop sign." He continued, "There is a gash on the side of her head and we had to free her leg from the pedals."

"Crap. Keep me informed," Morgan hung up the phone, sweat forming on his brow as he loosened his tie. His heart was pounding in his chest. He closed his eyes taking several deep breaths. Lifting his head, he hit the intercom button, "Gail tell the others that Rhea was in an accident, she is alive but we don't anymore."

He was on the phone reporting the incident to the head office when a message came through. 'She has been taken to The Eden Hospital.' Morgan pulled up his calendar for the rest of the day. Being so close to Christmas it was empty. He blanked out the rest of the day with the label 'Out of the Office'. Hanging up the phone he grabbed his bag and walked out.

Sitting in his car, he looked back at the hospital Emergency entrance, taking a deep breath as he fought to control his emotions. He walked up to the hospital reception and asked for Rhea's location. After a short phone call, the receptionist said, "She is in surgery.

Surgery. "Can you ring me when she is out," he handed over his business card.

Morgan paused at the hospital café. *Should I wait here?* Two patrons stared back at him. He looked down at his fire uniform. *I can't sit here all day looking like this. I will go home get changed and come back.*

Rhea is out of surgery. The hospital lift doors opened; Morgan hastened along the corridor. *Room 405.* He paused in the doorway taking a deep breath. A nurse was straightening the blanket on the bed. His pulse raced; the pain in his chest grew stronger with each step. Rhea lay motionless in the bed; her eyes closed, a bandage around her head. Her blonde hair mattered above the bandage. A deep red bruise merged with the scratches on the side of her head. Her lightly bandaged palms stopped him from taking hold of her hand. The bulge of her leg in plaster sticking out of the blankets made him turn away. *I think I'm going to be sick.* He turned to the nurse and quietly asked, "How is she?"

"Compound fracture of her lower right leg, bruising and a mild concussion." The nurse checked the drip bag, "We have her on sedatives. She will have a huge headache." Morgan nodded and turned back to Rhea as the nurse left the room.

He stood silent, head down staring at her battered body. Placing his hand on her arm, "You'll be all right," he murmured. He closed his eyes, clenching his jaw. *I was only dancing with her two days ago.* Tears welled in his eyes. *What can I do? Decades of rescue training but here I am useless.* Reaching into his pocket he pulled out his pen and scribbled a note on the card attached to his flowers. His pain grew as he stood there. "I'm sorry, I have to go."

The following morning, Morgan was weary from a lack of sleep; he pulled into the hospital carpark. Pulling out his phone he blocked out his calendar for the day. Grabbing the single rose off the passenger seat he headed for the elevator.

Her body hadn't changed. The bruising was a shade darker and the coloured tape on her bandages had changed from yellow to green. Taking a seat, he placed his hand on her arm and his forehead resting on the bed rail. *Why her? Please lord don't take her from me.* Tears trickled down his cheeks.

The sound of the clipboard hitting the end of the bed surprised him as he sat up. A nurse stood at the end of the bed, "I was going to let you sleep."

"I should be going," he leaned over gently kissing Rhea's uninjured cheek.

The following day, on Christmas Eve, Rhea was awake and feeling nothing as the drip kept the pain away. Her mother rearranged the flowers on the cupboard, "Look at all these. Someone must like you," she held up a piece of paper, "This one has a card." Handing the message to Rhea. She blinked to focus her eyes, *'Rhea, Get well soon. Morgan xx.'*

Morgan, that's nice. Holding the card to her chest, she fought to keep her eyes open. "She needs some sleep; we will come back later." Her mother's voice faded as everything went dark.

A few hours later she was awoken by the nurse wanting to do the regular check-up. Rhea closed her eyes as she was poked and prodded. Footsteps entered the room. "How is she going?" *Morgan.* His voice was soft. A renewed energy rose inside her as she opened her eyes. *He's looking a bit haggard.*

Her eyes locked on his as he stepped closer. "Morgan, it's good to see you."

"How are you feeling?"

"Stiff and numb."

His hand reached into his pocket pulling out a wrapped gift. It was flat and wrapped in red paper with a green ribbon. "Merry Christmas."

"Thank you but you didn't have to bring me a present."

"You're having a lousy Christmas. So, here's something to cheer you up." He leaned over lightly kissing her cheek.

"Thank you. I am going home this afternoon if you plan on visiting again."

His sombre face lit up. The touch of his hand was warm against her arm, "That's great." Reaching into his jacket pocket he pulled out his notebook and pen. He scribbled a note and handed it to her. "If you want to talk over Christmas, ring me."

"Thank you for the flowers. They are lovely."

He smiled back, the tears welling in his eyes made them sparkle. Taking a deep breath, he seemed to choke on his words. His focus was broken when the doctor walked in. "Well, I better go," he patted her arm before turning around. *He looked so conflicted as he rushed out the door.*

Rhea's parent returned later that afternoon, "The doctor rang and said we can take you home." They started packing everything. The collection of flowers had grown since their last visit, "We will need some more bags."

The sight of home eased some of the tension in Rhea's shoulders. Clambering out of the car and gaining her balance on the crutches was draining. She took a deep breath to regain her strength. Hobbling up her front steps with crutches was a skill she needed to master. Dropping down on the couch her leg ached. The sight of her mother cleaning the kitchen added to her agony. "Don't worry about that Mum."

"Are you sure you don't want to come back with us? You can have your old bedroom."

Rhea sighed, "No Mum, all my stuff is here and your place has too many stairs."

"Who is going to look after you?"

"I have a broken leg. And my mates drop over regularly," Rhea lifted her leg onto the couch. "Don't you have dinner at your sister's tonight?"

"What about dinner with you?"

"You are coming back here tomorrow morning for lunch. Isn't that enough?"

Dad looked back and nodded as he guided Mum to the door, "See you tomorrow, darling. Ring us if you need anything." *Dad is always the sensible one.*

The door closed and Rhea sighed. Dropping her head back on the armrest she closed her eyes. *Peace at last.* Her stress melted away with each breath. She went over what she could remember from the last few days. Her eyes sprung open. *He gave me a present.* Her pulse increased as she dug around in her bag pulling out the gift. Peeling back the paper, revealed a photo of them both dancing at the Christmas party. That long red dress, the hem draped across the floor and Morgan in his uniform. The warm feelings of him holding her as they swayed grew inside her. Turning the picture over, a message drew her focus. *'Love always Morgan xx.'* She held her breath for a moment, staring back at those words. *He loves me?*

Where have I seen this writing before? She pulled out her purse retrieving the Secret Santa message. *The handwriting is the same!* Her shoulders stiffened as her pulse increased. She placed the photo and message on the coffee table. Staring down at them both she remembered the times she had worked with him over the years. The courses, meetings, and incident responses. *When did his feelings start? Why didn't he say anything? Why didn't I notice anything? I guess I was always too busy to notice.*

Her stomach was in knots, she laid back staring at the photo. Her red dress stood out against his blue suit. That warm smile as he looked at the camera. *I always enjoyed his company. He always cheered me up when times were tough.* His words when he handed her the gift echoed in her head. *Something to cheer you up. I need some cheering up tonight.* She pulled out the phone number he gave her in the hospital. Holding the note up, her eyes drifted to the Secret Santa note. *It is the same paper; the same little logo in the corner and handwriting.* The words 'my feelings for you' stood out from the note. A lump developed in her throat. *I can't ring him; I work with him.* In her hand, the page with his phone number tempted her. *Oh, what the hell, he said to ring him.*

A short time later the doorbell rang. "Just a minute," She grabbed a crutch and pulled herself to her feet. Each hop jarred under her arms; she regained her balance as she adjusted her shirt. An excitement rose through her body as she opened the door. "Morgan, hi come in, I'm sorry the place is a mess."

He glanced back with a big smile, "Mess? You haven't seen the lunch room at work."

She dropped onto the couch; her eyes fixed on him as he crossed the room. *His dress shirt and slacks look fancy.* She looked down at her casual shirt and skirt.

In his hand was a full shopping bag. "What have you got there?"

"Some Mexican and Italian. I didn't know what you felt like."

"I could have cooked dinner." She strained to stand up.

"Stay there. You are meant to be resting." He went over to the kitchen grabbing some cutlery and two glasses.

She sighed; her eyes dropping to the floor. *I don't want him waiting on me.*

He sat in the seat near her and pulled out a wine bottle with the food.

"I can't have alcohol with these pain meds."

"I figured that, it's non-alcoholic. We will have to pretend it's real," he cracked the seal on the bottle.

Raising her glass, she said, "Cheers." She wriggled in the chair to face him more. "You didn't have to do this. Gail told me you cancelled your family holiday for me."

"I didn't cancel it; I postponed the ticket. It was just a family Christmas getaway in New Zealand."

"New Zealand, that makes me feel worse."

"I had to postpone it. The other Captain on duty had a car accident." His voice softened, "And I would not have enjoyed myself knowing you were home injured."

She pushed the note off the photo on the coffee table, "If you are going to write secret love letters. Don't use your natural handwriting."

His eyes rose to meet hers, and his cheeks reddening, "How did you work it out?"

"I'm a bloody trainer. I specialise in forensic handwriting. Have you seen how those students write?"

"Every time they send in an incident report." He glanced back with a smile, and then back to his dinner taking another mouthful.

"Anyone in your life?" She sipped her drink.

"No, my days of being chased by women are gone. They go after the younger recruits now."

She raised her eyebrows, "You're not that old. What are you? Thirty-five, forty?"

"I still made the calendar," he flashed his eyebrows and grinned. "Did you like the photo?"

"I haven't looked," she murmured.

"My feelings are hurt."

"I trained most of them, it felt creepy."

"Check out September. It's not just me it's a team photo with the fire truck."

"Having a half-naked photo of my co-worker on the wall isn't weird at all," she placed her empty dish on the table.

She sat silently; reading his body language as he finished his dinner. *I could do a lot worse than him. Stuff the work rules. They are not here.* She shuffled up the couch and patted the space beside her. "Come sit here." She reached over pressing a button on her mobile phone. "Some relaxation music." Slow jazz music drifted from the speakers near the TV.

He eased down beside her placing his arm on the backrest behind her. She leaned back nestling under his arm. His body felt warm, his touch reassuring. Her heart rate slowed as she felt the stress drifting away. She dropped her hand on his knee. "Thank you for coming over tonight. I needed cheering up."

"Anytime," he took hold of her hand. She dropped her head onto his chest. They sat silently enjoying each other's company while listening to the music.

Morgan lifted her hand and brought it to his warm lips. "I feared the worst when Jeff rang me from the accident. I'm glad you're OK."

"I'm glad I have your support." Her heart pounded in her chest. She twisted her body around. Her eyes ran up his chest pausing briefly at his soft lips before connecting with his warm brown eyes. Gently placing her palm on the side of his neck drawing him closer as her lips met his in a tender kiss. She dropped her gaze taking a deep breath. A moment later, he moved around placing his hand behind her head while edging closer, his warm lips caressing hers.

A warm grew inside her but trying to cuddle with a broken leg was awkward. She shuffled again, trying to place her leg on the coffee table to align with his body.

He pulled back, "Don't take this the wrong way. But would you be more comfortable if we talked in your bed?"

She nodded as she struggled to get up. He pulled her onto her good leg and helped her navigate the furniture. With his arm around her waist, she started to hop towards the bedroom when he slid his arm under her thighs and swept her off her feet. Her pulse started pounding as she took a firm hold of his broad shoulders. He carried her down the hall, sliding through the door and gently placing her on the bed.

Her face blushed as she looked back at him. "Now you are showing off."

"I didn't do all that rescue training for nothing," he stood in the doorway, "What do you want to drink?"

"Coffee and some water would be lovely."

Upon his return, he kicked off his shoes and jacket before lying beside her. On his side a foot away, his face looking back at hers. "Is this more comfortable?" His voice was soft and reassuring.

"Yes, thank you." The bedside lamp cast a warm glow over his face. Feeling safe with him by her side, she brushed her fingers over his cheek, "Merry Christmas."

"Merry Christmas," he smiled briefly. He silently looked back at her.

He seems distracted. "What are you thinking?"

"I'm wondering if I should go. I don't want to outstay my welcome." His low voice echoed his insecurity.

Placing her hand on his arm, "You are welcome to stay if you want. I enjoy your company."

The phone buzzed. Rhea reached out and grabbed it. Morgan was behind her with his arm draped over her waist. She ran her eyes over the bed, they were still on top of the covers wearing the same clothes they went to bed in. *He looks so peaceful asleep.* Looking at her phone, *Mum.* 'Merry Christmas, we will be over in an hour if you need anything.'

"Oh, crap," she tried to sit up without disturbing Morgan.

"What's up," he looked back from the pillow.

"How do you feel about meeting my parents?" She rolled back to face him, "They are an hour away."

He leaned over with a soft kiss, "Good morning."

"Good morning." She slid her hand down his arm as he rolled back.

"Do you have a problem with me meeting them?"

"No."

He climbed out of bed, "An hour, gives us time to freshen up and have breakfast."

She pushed off the bed to stand up, "Can you help me get ready for a shower?"

He looked back straight-faced, his eyes wide, "Excuse me?"

"Don't get excited. Tape a garbage bag over my plaster."

"Oh," he sighed.

With everything set, she was about to close the bathroom door when she leaned towards him, "Can you start breakfast?"

She hobbled into the kitchen in time to see Morgan place a plate of bacon and eggs on the table. "Hope this meets your needs."

"It's great, thank you."

With breakfast over, Rhea checked her watch. "They will be here soon." The knot in her chest grew as she thought about her mother meeting him for the first time. Hurrying to clean up on one crutch took effort. Morgan cleaned the dishes; that job requires two hands. She was wiping the bench when a car pulled up at the front of the house. Rhea turned towards Morgan, "Now is your time to bail if you want to."

He stood before her, wrapping his arms around her waist, "It will be all right. We are trained to handle disasters."

"It better not be a bloody disaster. I have had enough of those for a while."

He returned a quick kiss as the doorbell buzzed. "I'll get it."

"Coming," Rhea called out.

The door opened and both parents paused looking at Morgan and then back to Rhea.

Rhea hobbled to the door, "This Morgan, we work together. He just dropped by to check on me."

After introductions, Morgan grabbed his coat, "Well I'll leave you in their capable hands. I'll call you later." He smiled as he walked out the door.

Lunch was over, and her parents had left but only after her mother had cleaned up. Drained from the morning Rhea collapsed on the couch. Stretched out with her hands under her cheek she stared down at the dance photo on the coffee table. A fire inside her wanted to get out, there were things she had to say. *Everything has changed I can't hold back anymore.* Grabbing her notebook, her gaze fixed on the empty page. The words started to flow uncontrollably as her pen ran across the page.

'Dearest Morgan, I always felt safe in your soulful eyes. Your warm heart gave me the courage to fight on. You were always there for me. I just never knew why until I woke in the hospital. Your guardian angel was watching over me. And I never want either of you to leave my side. Love always Rhea xx.'

Reading back the words made her heart heavy. Lowering the notebook, tears rolled down her face. Closing the book, she wiped her cheeks. *I can't let him see this.*

Later that evening, Rhea's phone rang. *Morgan.* "Hi, do you want to get out of the house and grab some dinner?"

"Sounds good."

"Pick you up in an hour."

59

Sitting in the outdoor dining area at the pub, the multicoloured Christmas lights still hung overhead. Rhea enjoyed her Chicken Parmi and soft drink. *Morgan seems to be enjoying his steak.* Her eyes roamed the crowd before coming back to connect with his.

"What's the problem?" He asked.

"Just thinking, what if someone sees us out together."

"We work together. What's wrong with taking your injured workmate out for Christmas?" He laid down his cutlery, "Do you worry every time you and Gail go to lunch."

"That's different."

"They don't know that. Now enjoy your meal."

After dinner they stood beside his car in the carpark, "I would normally suggest a walk on the beach but I don't think you are up for that." He opened her door, "Do you want to have a cruise up the coast for a bit?"

"That would be nice."

The car cornered smoothly on the coastal road. The leather interior was soft to the touch. "Nice car."

"What are you going to do for transport now?" His focus was on the road as he changed the gears.

"It's in the hands of the insurance company. I won't be able to drive for a while anyway."

"I can pick you up for work," he paused, "When are you cleared to go back to work?"

"Anytime, I am cleared for a desk job. The others will have to do the courses."

The car slowed as he turned into a roadside carpark near a lookout. Away from the city, everything was dark. The rising moon reflected off the lighter sandy footpath leading down to the lookout. She hobbled over to a concrete picnic table. "I need to sit down."

Morgan stood before her and wrapped his hands around her wrist lifting her onto the tabletop, "You can see more from up there." He climbed up onto the table tucking his body behind her. Sliding a leg on each side of her hips, he wrapped his arms around her shoulders.

The moonlight sparkled on the ocean waves. Her long hair fluttered in the sea breeze. She tucked it into her jacket to keep it out of his face. His warmth surrounded her shutting out the cool ocean wind. She closed her eyes, taking slow breaths as her stress melted away. His gentle touch made her feel secure. *This feels good.* Taking hold of his hands, her thumbs slowly brushed his skin. "Did you mean what you said in the Secret Santa note?"

"Every word," he climbed off the table, standing between her legs. Face to face in the darkness she could feel his warm breath on her cheek. His fingers gently brushed her neck as he pushed back her hair. The darkness heightened her senses, his touch sent a shiver down her back. She wrapped her arms around his chest drawing his body closer to hers. His soft lips caressed hers in a long slow kiss. Her pulse increased as her hands ran through his hair. She took a breath as she moved her broken leg. The throbbing pain was killing her mood. Pulling back, "Let's continue this at home, where it is more comfortable."

The first day back at work since her accident. Rhea's uniform had changed to a skirt as she couldn't get her leg plaster in her standard work pants.

Morgan pulled up at the office entrance, "Have a good day, I'll call you later."

"I so want to kiss you."

"Later," he smiled as he pushed the button to open her door.

The lift doors opened and Rhea had worked out how to move at speed on crutches. It was quiet in the office as most of the staff were still on holiday. Gail greeted her with a hug.

Taking a seat at her desk, everything was clean and tidy. Rhea glanced at her inward document tray; it usually groaned with files but sat empty. *Were they expecting me back this week?* She turned on her computer, the emails were few as most of the offices were still closed but one email stood out. The Regional Commander wanted a meeting when she returned. Her pulse started racing. *What does the boss want from me?*

She knocked on his door, he jumped up to open it for her. *He seems happy enough; it can't be too bad.* "You wanted to see me." She leaned on her crutches.

"Take a seat." He handed her an envelope and a set of epaulettes.

Every muscle froze as her eyes widened. She scanned the label on the envelope, *Director of Training Rhea Dempsy. Director?* "What's this?"

"Your promotion. It starts in two weeks. You'll spend the next few weeks getting training from the retiring director."

Her hands started to tremble; she took a deep breath to control her nerves. "Thank you," she started for the door when the Commander stepped up, he reaching out removing her current epaulettes and replacing them with the new ones. "Congratulations, Director Dempsy."

A cold sweat broke out on her brow. Hurrying back to her desk her pulse was pounding in her head. In the past whenever she was this stressed, she would call Morgan. His soothing voice would ease her nerves. Holding her phone in front of her she took a selfie. *I could have looked better for a promotion pic.* She attached it to a text message, 'Morgan, can you spot the difference?' Followed by a photo of the letter.

Her phone buzzed, "Congratulations. Well, I better have a meeting with the new Director of Training. Pick you up at lunch."

Another day over, Rhea paused at the end of the pool, taking several deep breaths. Her leg cast had been removed two weeks ago and she had to rebuild the muscles. Swimming was not as jarring as other exercises. She looked up at the clock. *I have time for a couple more laps.* Taking a deep breath, she set off again.

Pulling up at the blocks, she removed her goggles. She wiped the water from her face, as a tall fireman came through the entrance. *Morgan, right on time.* She pulled herself onto the side of the pool.

He crouched down handing her a towel. "Don't wear yourself out, we have dinner tonight."

Dinner? Oh, Valentine's Day. I forgot about that.

Back home, she limped out of the shower leaning on one crutch. Morgan casually sat at the end of her bed. Rhea pushed aside clothes in her wardrobe, "What am I going to wear?"

"I like the red dress."

"The dress I wore to the ball? That is too fancy for a pub dinner. And I have to wear my heels with it so I don't trip over the hem."

"So?"

"You want me in four-inch heels when I can't put weight on my ankle?"

"Go with the black dress then," he got up and left the bedroom.

Reaching for her notebook she tore out the letter she had written on Christmas Day placing it in an envelope. She looked back at the letter. *Should I give it to him tonight?*

Walking past the mirror she checked her hair and makeup. "I'm ready," her eyes were drawn to a big bunch of red roses sitting on the counter. Below the bunch, an envelope rested against the vase.

"Happy Valentine's Day," he reached over with a hug.

"Thank you," she picked up the envelope, "What's this another cryptic note?" She slid out a folded piece of paper and two airline tickets. Her jaw dropped, "New Zealand."

"Well, I'm not going over there by myself." He stood next to her, "Read the note."

A three-night stay at Matakauri Lodge Queenstown at the start of the ski season. Her eyes connected with his, "Do you ski? I can't."

"No, but there are other things we can do there."

"Yes, there are." She smiled leaning in for a kiss.

Collecting her purse, they headed out the door. She turned to him, "You will have to wait till after dinner for your present."

Later that night, Rhea, lay next to Morgan, her head on his chest and her arm holding him close. The thud of his heartbeat reverberated in her ear. He rolled over, his face filling her vision as he caressed her lips one more time. "I have an early start tomorrow; I'll get Gail to pick you up."

"You can stay if you want to."

"I'm easily distracted here. I need some sleep."

Opening the door, the street was quiet and dark. He stepped through the door, reaching back for a hug and kiss good night. Rhea pulled an envelope from her pocket, placing it in his hand. "Don't open it here."

"Good night."

Her eyes followed him down the stairs to his car. Closing the door, she stepped to the side peering out the window. He climbed into his car; the headlights came on as the engine started. She turned back towards the kitchen. A moment later, the doorbell buzzed. *Has he forgotten something?*

He took no time stepping through the door, shutting it with a kick. With tears in his eyes, he threw his arms around her. His grip was firm as he lifted her feet off the floor. Letting go only to cradle her head in his palms, drawing her in for a passionate kiss. Wrapping his arms around her shoulders he squeezed her body against his and didn't let go.

"I said not to read it here," she mumbled with her face squashed against his shoulder.

It's July already, my first chance to have a holiday since becoming the Director of Training. Rhea stared out the bus window as it left Queenstown behind. Snow-capped mountains surrounded the crystal blue lake. She pulled up her collar with anticipation of the cold wind at the resort. *What a crazy year it has been; the unexpected promotion, the rehabilitation after my accident, Morgan, and another basic*

firefighter course completed. I missed the hands-on training. As Director I never had the time to sit in on this last class.

Morgan tapped her arm, "Smile."

She glanced back to have another photo taken. "You will fill up that memory card before we get there."

"I have two more cards."

The resort room was hidden among the lush gardens. Swiping the access card, she paused in the doorway, the room was huge. Warm colours matched by the crackling fire making the room toasty. *The lounge suite is bigger than my home lounge room.* A large king-size bed sat behind a curtain wall.

"Check out this bathroom."

A large porcelain bath sat in front of a large picture window. The views were all lake and alps.

"Do we have to leave?" She leaned against him, wrapping her arms around his hips.

"Our pay wouldn't cover the rent."

The following morning, Rhea was shopping when Morgan pulled up with a hire car. Loading the bags in the back, she slipped into the passenger seat. "What are we going to do with this?"

"Site seeing, get some photos," handing her a tourist pamphlet, "Work out what you want to see."

She flicked through the pages, "What do you want to see?"

"The Sunset from a lookout around the point."

It was getting late in the afternoon. Morgan was busy loading the car with his camera bag. After a quick run along the bay, they pulled into the carpark. The lookout was a short walk from the carpark. Rhea stopped at the railing, Morgan by her side. His arm behind her back; the sun slowly sinking behind the snow-capped mountains. The shades of white and blue were replaced with pink and orange. Warm colours changed constantly as the light faded. The sky was illuminated by fiery orange clouds topped with mauve. Another couple stood over further taking photos of everything. Rhea glanced over to Morgan's chest; his camera hung motionless. *He has been taking photos this whole trip.*

"Aren't you taking photos of the sunset?"

He dropped his arm, "Yeah, right." Her eyes fixed on the mountain peaks. Morgan shuffled around beside her. The woman from the other group sat on a rock nearby turning her music up as she stared over the lake. A soft ballad wafted on the breeze. *At least she likes good music.*

"Rhea." Morgan's deep voice softened.

Looking back at him, he took her hand and dropped to a knee. Her eyes widened as she held her breath. *Is he?* Her eyes locked on him as the surrounding world disappeared.

"You wrote in your letter, that you didn't want me to leave your side. I don't want to leave your side. Rhea Dempsy, will you marry me?" In his hand a diamond solitaire ring framed in white gold. Each facet glistened with the last rays of sunshine.

With a deep gasp, "Yes." Every nerve was alive, her inner voice was screaming.

She reached out her trembling hand. He tenderly held it still as he slid the ring on her finger.

A tear ran down her cheek as she threw her arms around his shoulders. His hand in the middle of her back pulled her body closer; his determined lips confirmed his intentions as they met hers. Arm in arm his love was as strong as his embrace. She rested her head on his chest as she looked out over the water.

"Look this way please."

Rhea glanced over her shoulder at the guy pointing his camera at them snapping photos constantly. *What the?*

Morgan turned towards the guy, wrapping his arms around Rhea, "Smile."

As the camera clicked, the guy's shirt logo became clearer, *Glenn's Photographic Studio. I thought the camera looked expensive for a tourist. He hired a photographer. How much planning did he put into this?*

"You could have told me to wear something better than a ski jacket." She whispered, taking different poses.

"Where's the secret in that?"

"Face each other," the photographer danced around getting different angles.

Her arms were over his shoulders. His hands on her hips. Staring deeply into his soul made the electricity rise inside her. Closing her eyes she leaned in for a loving kiss.

Back home Rhea looked over the photos of that evening. *The light was all but gone, the last few photos were the two of us embracing. Entwined dark silhouettes against a golden glow framed by the mountains across the lake. I will have to find something for the wedding to beat that proposal.*

The End of Story 3.

SHORT STORY 4

FIRESIDE

Contemporary Christmas Romance

Written By C. L. Hamilton

4. FIRESIDE

A leisurely hike in the hills had turned into an endurance race for the Singles Girls Christmas tour. Sonia's heart was pumping. She slid down the slippery slopes as rocks rolled from under her feet. *A relaxing day out they said.* She stopped to wipe the sweat from her eyes as the younger members jogged off into the distance.

Dean the tour guide was the last in the line, "Hold up in front." Pulling up beside Sonia, "Are you OK? We have to keep going." The late afternoon light darkened as storm clouds rolled over the ridge line. Distant thunder rattled through the hills. The far-off peaks slowly vanished in a white veil. Her heart skipped a beat each time a sheet of lightning flashed across the sky.

Finally, at the bottom of the slope, Sonia bent over gasping for air. The gentle trickle of the creek ahead had developed more of a roar. Taking a deep breath, she looked ahead, the flat path followed the bank. Dean darted into the scrub towards the creek bank, returning a minute later.

"The water is rising fast. We won't get back to the bridge before it goes under." Dean called out to those further down the track, "Take the track to your right."

The thunder and ground strikes were getting closer. Each boom made Sonia flinch. She took off after the others when a blinding flash of light came from behind. A sonic boom filled the air all around her. *Crap. I'm going to die.* The cold rain pelted down turning the dirt into greasy mud underfoot. Reaching the creek bank, the water had become a churning chocolate milkshake topped with brown foam. Everyone came to a sudden stop.

"A tree. Who are we, Indiana Jones?" The front hiker asked.

A large tree had fallen across the creek at some point in history. It had been turned into a bridge with a rope handrail on one side.

"Move!" Dean yelled to be heard over the thunder.

Five of the hikers stood on the other side of the creek. Sonia looked across the log before staring at the water below. Her heart raced, as every muscle in her body screamed no. The hikers were cheering her on from the other side.

"You can do this," Dean placed his hand on her shoulder to comfort her nerves.

Taking a firm grip on the rope she shuffled one foot in front of the other. Partway along the log, the far end of the tree dropped a short distance. *Crap!* Sonia wobbled trying to keep balance. The far bank then completely gave way, and the end of the trunk fell into the swirling water. Sonia up to her chest in flowing water gripped the rope tight. "Dean!" Her panic rang out as each finger slipped around the rope.

The flow had a firm grip on her body as it dragged her under. She gasped for air in the icy water.

"Sonia!" Dean called out as she disappeared under the water. "Get help!" He yelled at the other hikers. With his eyes fixed on her last location, he jumped onto the trunk below and into the water. Fighting the current he felt around trying to find her under the water. With all his focus on locating her and staying alive, he ignored the passing debris hitting his body.

He scanned the creek, finding Sonia caught on a fallen tree in the middle of the water. Struggling with the current he finally reached her. The terror grew on her face as he tried to pry her hands free of the branch. "We have to get out of this water." Taking a firm grip on her waist, they battled the current as they headed for the nearby bank.

Rising to the surface a distance downstream Dean clung onto a tree branch near the water's edge. Gasping for air he heaved Sonia onto the tree beside him. She was conscious and her body shook all over. *I have to warm her up.*

The rain was getting heavier and the lightning enclosed the hills. Pulling her ashore he panned the terrain. *Where am I? That's Dawson's Peak, there should be a hut not far from here.*

He gasped for air, and his heart pounded in his chest. *I have to get her out of here.* She was leaning against his legs, her body trembling in the mud. He dragged her to her feet and grabbed her waist. With her arm over his shoulders, he fought off his shivering as he stumbled through the undergrowth.

Reaching the track, he paused to catch his breath before he picked up the pace. *Cabin to the right, let's go.*

Pushing open the door, he laid her on the floor next to the fireplace. His aching muscles wanted to join her. *I have to get the fire started. Great they have restocked the wood pile.*

The rain on the tin roof got louder and the temperature dropped. *It's bloody December. They forecast heat waves for Christmas, yet we are shivering.* He dug into his soggy day pack for his emergency fire kit. A few strikes of the fire rod and he had fire. Looking back at Sonia she was huddled in a ball, with every muscle shivering. Her skin had gone pale and cold.

After ripping off his wet shirt and pants he hung them on the wood pile to dry. In his boxer shorts, he crouched beside Sonia, "You have hypothermia. You have to remove your wet clothes." He hesitantly started with her shoes. His chest was in knots as he fought his nerves. *She will die of hypothermia if I don't warm her up.* But he was hesitant about removing a female stranger's clothes. She was conscious and provided some help getting her arms out of the shirt. Finally, down to her underwear, he wrapped her in the foil emergency blanket in his kit.

It didn't take long for the cabin to warm up. Sonia stopped shaking as she started to improve. The storm continued outside as the wind howled past the windows drowned out by random claps of thunder.

"We are not going anywhere tonight," he murmured as he curled up beside her.

Sonia lay awake staring at the flickering flames. Her body ached from the afternoon's turn of events. She rolled over, the hard wooden floor pushing on her hips made her discomfort worse. *What is the use of a survival cabin if it doesn't have a bed?*

Today did not go to plan. We booked a relaxing mountain hike as part of the tour. We were all given day packs, each kitted out with supplies and water for the trip. Her eyes darted around the room. *I don't know where my kit ended up. I had it when I fell into the water. I can't remember much after that. There is a vague memory of him pulling me up the slope. He saved me.* Her body started trembling as tears formed in her eyes. *I would be dead now if it weren't for him diving into the creek.*

Her eyes drifted over to Dean lying on the floor with his back to her. Wearing nothing but his boxer shorts, the fire's glow highlighted every rippling muscle on his ribs. The silhouette of his broad shoulders and biceps stood out against the flames. *He dragged me from the river, he had to be fit. But he must like adventure. Why else would a tall good-looking hiking guide lead a group of six single women into the wild?* While the sight in front of her was interesting it was not enough to overcome her pain.

She groaned, sitting up as the floorboards added to her agony. Dean rolled over towards her, "Are you all right?"

"I can't sleep. How are you?"

"I'll survive."

Her leg stung as the numbing cold faded. Looking down in the dim light she had a graze on her shin. *I don't remember getting that.*

She wrapped her arms around her legs as she huddled before the fire, tears building in her eyes. Her body gently rocked as a tear ran down her face. She buried her face in her arms as she fought off her emotions of the day.

Dean slid towards her placing his arm over her back, "What's the problem?"

"If it weren't for you, I would be dead now." She briefly connected with his gaze, but the humanity in his eyes was overwhelming. Tears rolled down her cheeks as she dropped her gaze to the floor.

He reached out with a reassuring hug. His embrace was warm and calming. "I wasn't going to let you drown in the river." Sitting back up, he wiped the tears from her face.

"Thank you. Do you have anything to eat, I lost my kit."

Turning around he pulled out two plastic bags from his kit, "Nuts or raspberry lollies?"

Huddled together they had their limited dinner. "Why are you on a wilderness adventure two days before Christmas?" Dean asked, "Most people are heading for their families."

"It's part of the single girls' Christmas in the Outback tour. Mountain hiking before spending Christmas at the Blue Hills Country Retreat," she replied. "Why are you wandering the bush two days before Christmas?"

"It's a job and gets me out of the city," he leaned over and tossed another log on the fire.

"Why don't you join us at the lodge for Christmas dinner?"

He turned his head, his eyebrows raised, "A room full of single women drinking alcohol and partying. Are you trying to kill me?"

She chuckled, "Don't tell the girlfriend."

He reached for his drink bottle. "I know what you are doing?"

She looked back at his face with a coy smile. "Well, I like to get to know a guy before he sees my underwear."

"I like to know a woman before I sleep with them too," he replied. "If it weren't for this fire I would have been forced to go full survival. Both of us naked under that blanket."

Her chest tightened as that image ran through her head. Silently staring back at him she wrapped the blanket around herself tighter.

"That got you thinking," he replied handing her the water bottle.

Taking a mouthful of water, she went back to staring at the fire. "You didn't answer my question. Do you have a girlfriend?" She asked, "Are you in trouble for spending the night with a woman in the wild?"

"I'm single. And I would rather my night spent in a cabin with a woman was better than this."

"What would you prefer?"

"Food, wine, somewhere comfy to sleep."

As time went on the questions kept flowing. His eyes grew heavy. She could feel her energy drained. "Let's get some sleep," she laid down beside him.

The first beams of light came in the window. The room was getting colder as the last flame died leaving a few embers behind. Sonia awoke to find herself tucked up against Dean's warm back with her arm over his waist. The foil blanket partly covered them both. *Oh crap.* Easing away she tried not to wake him; she slowly slid her arm back.

At the first movement of her hand, "Good morning," he said without moving.

She jolted back, "I'm sorry."

"Survival 101," he yawned while turning over.

She locked eyes with him, "But—"

"Relax. Nothing happened. You got cold and moved closer that's all." He stood up taking his dry clothes from the wood pile. Shoving his arm into the sleeve he peered out the window. "The storm has cleared up. It's light enough for us to get back to camp."

"Can you throw me my clothes?" She asked still wrapped in the blanket.

He grabbed the last of his gear. Handing her clothes to her as he headed for the door, "I'll get dressed outside. Hurry up they have probably started to search for us."

Dressed in her dry clothes she sat down to put on her shoes. "Ewww," she groaned as her feet slipped into the cold soggy boots.

Dean called out through the wall, "Are you dressed? I hear motorbikes."

Motorbikes. She picked the pace by shoving her laces inside her boots. The bikes pulled up outside. Upon opening the door Dean was already talking to the police search team.

He swung his leg over the back of one of the bikes, "Get on."

She stood frozen staring back at him. "I've never been on a motorbike."

"Or you can walk the five kilometres back to camp," Dean replied.

Five kilometres. Her aching body screamed no. She swung her leg over the bike, gripping the rider's waist tightly.

With the last question answered the police started to pack up. An ambulance officer bandaged their wounds. "Have your doctor check them when you get to town."

The tour group sat around the four-wheel drive waiting for their guide to take them back to town. If they were concerned, they weren't showing it now, drinking coffee and chatting.

Sonia walked around behind the police van, looking at the ground. *This trip has been a disaster. It was meant to be a fun getaway in nature.* The feelings of fear when she fell into the water came flooding back. Her hands started to shake and tears filled her eyes. *I could have died.*

Dean stuck his head around the corner of the van. "There you are."

She didn't reply. He stood in front of her, "Can I help with anything?"

She reached out wrapping her arms around with a warm hug, "Thank you for saving my life."

"Anytime," he replied.

They stood arm in arm, her head resting on his shoulder. Her grip was firm. Her breathing slowed as her body relaxed.

"Are you ready to leave?" He asked with concern.

She nodded, "See you at Blue Hills?"

"I will see what I can do."

Up in the mountains, the cool breeze blew across the valley. The heatwave warnings on the coast were a distant problem. Sonia and her new friends sat on the deck overlooking the Blue Hill pastures. She leaned back soaking up the sun as she sipped her pineapple juice. The Christmas celebrations started at lunch. Waiters keep asking if they want more drinks and bringing around food platters. *Just how much do they think we can eat in one day?*

The gardens were laced with party lights and decorations for the night ahead. A line of roasting spits and bar-b-ques simmered away outside of catering. Smells of roast dinner drifted on the breeze. Christmas carols, old and new softly play in the background. The catering company continued to set up the tables under the marques. A mini loader piled up wood for the bonfire.

Sonia's two friends left to have a snooze before dinner. She sat quietly looking over the countryside. Black and white cows were randomly dotted over the green slopes. A group of tourists on horseback disappeared over the rise. *What am I going to do this afternoon? I might go for a walk and talk to the animals.*

Someone dropped down into the seat beside her, "Didn't think they were going to leave."

What the? "Dean. You made it." *Wow, he has changed.* The rugged mountain guide covered in sweat and dirt scrubbed up well. *Not sure if I like the stubble or the clean-shaven version.* A clean button-up shirt and jeans replaced the muddy kaki survival outfit.

"What are you up to?" He reached out and grabbed a handful of crackers.

"I'm going for a walk."

"Sounds good," he reached for another handful for the walk.

Heading down the gravel path towards the animal enclosures. She asked, "Are you staying the night?"

"Yeah. I'm planning on having a few drinks."

"What room are you in?"

"Couldn't get a room, they were booked out," he said, "I have my camper parked in the camping area over there." Pointing to a mown field dotted with tents and camper vans.

"I'm sharing a room with two other women," she grinned, "Don't get ideas."

"Three women, hell no."

Walking past the chicken coop brought them all running. Every human was a potential source of food. Sonia stopped at the horse paddock to pat a fat horse. It seemed to have the same belief as the chickens. Scratching the horse's side, she looked back at Dean, "What do you do for a job?"

"I'm self-employed running a tour group."

"Tours where?"

"Anywhere. They are paying for it. What do you do?"

"Administration in a furniture warehouse," she said patting the horse before wandering on further.

With dinner over the party moved into the paddock, sitting around the raging bonfire and having fun. Drunkard carollers and dancers cheering made talking difficult. Dean leaned over to Sonia's ear, "Do you want to come back to my campfire? It will be quieter."

Coming out of the darkness, his camp was set up with more luxury than the cabin at the hike. The back of his four-wheel drive included a bed inside the cabin and a pull-out annex on the side. The tray was lined with draws containing everything including the kitchen sink.

"Take a seat," Dean said pointing to a log beside the campfire.

Sitting on the ground using the log as a backrest she stared into the everchanging flames. The rising sparks circled in the wind overhead before disappearing. A distant sound of cheering filtered down the slope occasionally. Dean leaned over the log, "What do you want to drink?"

"Anything will do?"

Handing her an ice-cold beer, he headed back to the camper. On his return, he sat next to her, placing a blanket beside him. He glanced back at her as he reached under the blanket, "Merry Christmas."

He held up a shoebox-sized present. Her eyes widened as she looked back at him. "I didn't get you anything."

"Don't worry about that."

Peeling back the wrapper, she held up a survival kit for a belt. "Wow, that's great. You didn't have to do that."

"Open it."

Lifting the flap, a note covered the contents. She ran her eyes down the page. "A free week of one-on-one outback touring at a destination of your choice.

"Thank you." She leaned over for a friendly hug. "You could have given this to me tomorrow."

"I didn't know if I would see you tomorrow. You all could be off horse riding and hitting on some rugged cowboy."

"I can't ride," she sipped her beer. "It's going to be chilly tonight."

Dean pulled the blanket over them, "Is that better?"

Huddled under the blanket Sonia kept pulling the edge of the blanket over her legs.

"You can get closer," Dean held out his arm, inviting her to cuddle.

"Are you sure?" She asked hesitantly.

"Yes. We have been half-dressed alone in a cabin while you spooned me," he said, "I think this is pretty tame."

Moving in closer, he lowered his arm over her shoulders. His warm body nestled against hers. Resting her head on his shoulder, she stared at the crackling fire. She could hear his pulse bounding strong and steady.

"You haven't asked if I have a boyfriend?"

"You're on a single girl's tour. What boyfriend would be happy about that?"

Well, he pays attention. Adjusting to be more comfortable she placed her arm across his ribs.

"You didn't have to give me the tour voucher. The kit was more than enough."

"I don't want you going away saying you almost died on my tour," he replied placing his hand on hers.

"Did you give the others vouchers?"

"No, they didn't fall in the creek," he said, "And I only wanted to see one of you again."

See one of us. Her heart skipped a beat as she sat silently relaxing in his warm embrace. The flames brought her back to their first night in the cabin, the hike seemed like such a long time ago.

"Where would you like to go on your next tour?"

"Someplace with warm water. Natural. Maybe a tropical island."

"So, you want to see me again?"

She sat up, her eyes connecting with his, "I will have to wait till I have holidays again. Could be the middle of the year."

"No problem."

"Don't go celibate waiting for me."

"I don't sleep with a different woman on each tour."

"You know what I mean." Her words were drowned out by

fireworks and the partygoers all yelling, "Merry Christmas." Their voices echoed across the valley.

He glanced at his watch, "Midnight. Merry Christmas." His voice was soothing as he leaned his head on hers.

Looking back at his warm smile, she slowly moved closer, "Merry Christmas." Her lips met his with a loving kiss. Glancing back before she snuggled back against his chest, pulling the blanket higher.

The cool breeze flickered the flames. Dean shuffled out from the blanket, "I'm having a cup of coffee. Do you want a drink? Tea, coffee, beer?"

"Coffee is good."

The kettle was heating on the gas cooker, and he was digging around the drawers when Sonia came up behind him wrapped in the blanket, "Do you have a permanent home or is this your home?"

"This is my home for most of the year. During the down times, I camp at my brother's place."

"Don't you get tired of always moving?"

"I have no reason to be tied to one place," he poured the hot water into the cups, "Being single I most well see the country at someone else's expense."

How is this going to work? It would be like dating a spy. I'd never know where he was from one minute to the next. Taking her cup, she headed back towards the fire.

"You can camp in the van if you don't want to sleep with the others," Dean said, "I can camp near the fire."

Her cold hands wrapped around the hot cup. "If you want to see me again. How am I meant to find you?"

"Ring my business number, it's the only number I have," he replied, "If I'm out of range, leave a message."

"Do you think this will work?" She looked up as he sat beside her.

He moved closer placing his arm behind her back, "It's early days. Things can change," he said, "I have your number on file, I can call you when I'm in range. If I'm close enough I can drop in and say hello."

Part-time boyfriend. The flames slowly gave way to glowing embers as she had her last mouthful of coffee. "Is the camper offer still on?"

"Sure," he got up heading for the van. "I'll grab my swag."

She came up beside him, "You don't have to sleep near the fire."

With swag in hand, he looked back, "Are you sure?"

"It's not our first time sleeping in the same room. And we have clothes on this time."

Climbing up into the van, the double bed was cosy. His warmth was only inches away. Lying on her back, a small lamp lit up the food packets on the shelf over the bed. *Is this ever going to work?* "Good night," she murmured.

He leaned over softly placing his palm on the side of her head, his face moving closer with each breath. She closed her eyes as his warm lips met hers. Moving back her eyes locked with his as she grasped his neck, caressing his lips in a passionate kiss. She lightly gripped his hair as he nuzzled her neck. The regrowth on his chin tickled her bare skin as goosebumps rose over her body. They rolled over, she looked up at him before she grabbed his biceps pulling him towards her. He paused as he looked back at her before leaning down with a long slow kiss.

She woke the following morning to find herself alone in the van. *Where has he gone?* Her bare shoulders were cool from the night air. *I better get dressed.* Clothed, she stretched as she climbed out of the camper and scanned the area. He was coming back from the country house carrying something. Pushing back her mattered hair she took a seat near the dead fire.

He handed her a plate of everything on the breakfast buffet. "Good morning," he leaned over with a morning kiss.

Looking at the pile of food, "Thanks. I don't eat this much."

"I didn't know what you wanted."

With breakfast over, she gathered her Christmas present, turning to Dean, "My bus leaves in half an hour."

He wrapped his arms around her shoulders, drawing her nearer. "I will call when I can. I have enjoyed our time together."

"Leave out the almost drowning bit," she replied.

"I'm sorry."

"Don't worry about it. I have to go get my gear."

"I'll walk you back."

Walking up the slope he had her bag over his shoulder; hand in hand, he said, "I'm going to miss you."

"Well, you know where to find me."

She stood back watching the last of the luggage being loaded into the bus. "Got to go," she reached out for a last hug.

His soft lips met hers, before he whispered in her ear, "Till I see you again."

She silently boarded the bus, looking back at him as he waved and headed into the trees.

Back home, it was New Year's Eve, Sonia dialled Dean's number and it went to the message bank. "Hey Dean, just touching base. Happy New Year's Eve."

The clock struck twelve and the phone stayed silent. "Happy New Year" she muttered sculling the last of her wine.

Her holiday was over, she was back to stocktakes and sales deliveries. When a co-worker asked about her Christmas holiday, she replied, "Just a tour with the girls."

Later that week, her phone buzzed several times during a meeting. Flicking it to silent she went back to listening to the boss talking. Stretching her legs at lunch, she checked her messages. *'Hi Sonia, it's Dean. I have been up in the mountains with my brother. Sorry, I missed you. I'll call later.'*

At home after dinner, Sonia climbed into bed reaching for her light when the phone rang. *Dean.* "Hello."

"Hey, how have you been?" He asked.

"Busy with work, usual stuff. What's happening with you?"

"Good and bad news. I have a big-ticket tour going up the coast. It's twelve weeks of travelling everywhere." He said, "It's a lot of money, but I will be out of phone range in places."

"That's great. Ring when you can." She replied, "I don't know when I'm getting holidays. I have an early morning. We will talk when you're able." *It's good to hear his voice but I'm wasting my time with him.*

Four months later and another day at work. A courier walked up to the desk handing her an envelope. 'Private - Sonia Boulton' was written across the letter. From D M Ford Tours. *Who is that?*

Peering into the envelope revealed an open airline ticket and a folded letter. *'Hi Sonia, I have found the tour location you wanted. I have set up a base in Proserpine, north Queensland. There are numerous islands off the coast, plus endless other places we can go. No more travelling across the country. You know where I am if you still want that tour. Cheers Dean.'*

Pulling up the map on her computer. *Proserpine? That's the other end of the country. He's making seeing me again difficult. Well, he has sent me a plane ticket.* Flicking to her calendar she scanned the months ahead. Looking back at the photos on the screen, the tropical beaches and ocean views raised her excitement for the rest of the day.

Mid-May the wet season was all but gone. Sonia waited for her bags at the Mackay airport. She leaned over to grab her suitcase when someone reached in and lifted her bag off the belt beside her. She spun around, "Part of the service."

"Dean." His smooth voice sounded happier than it had on the phone. His sparkling blue eyes matched his beaming smile. The same friendly face, the stubble had returned and his skin tanned from the months of tropical sun.

He placed her bags on the floor; he wrapped his arms around her. A warm embrace with a kiss on her cheek. "Welcome to north Queensland."

It wasn't hard to spot his vehicle in the carpark; a four-wheel drive decked out with every off-road mod and D M Ford Tours plaster along the side. *There must be money in this.*

Heading out of town he placed his hand on hers, "I'm glad you came. I didn't know if I would see you again."

"I felt the same when I left on the bus at the country retreat."

"Well, it's great that you're here. Let's have fun."

Summer had officially ended but the air was still warm and humid. The trip up to Proserpine in the air-conditioning revealed a landscape of green everywhere. A mixture of towering sugar cane, grasslands, and tropical forest as far as the eye could see.

Proserpine came and went as he turned off the main highway. "Where are we going?" Sonia asked.

"Airlie Beach. I bought a place there."

The beach, wow. "Have you been busy?" She stared out the passenger window at the tropical gardens passing by. A picture of a deep blue sky above a green landscape with flashes of colour, frangipanis, and palm trees.

"Yeah, but the tourist season hasn't started here yet."

"Why hasn't it?"

"The winter cold chases them up from down south. And Summer is too hot and humid plus cyclones scare them away."

After a short trip along a dirt track, he pulled up in front of an older-style timber house hidden among the shrubs and palm trees. Tucked away in the bushland backing onto the hills. Numerous birds chirped in the trees. She scanned the horizon, "Where's the beach?"

"A couple of kilometres down the road. I couldn't afford a waterfront property," he unlocked the front door. "Just how rich do you think I am?"

The bright interior was fresh and clean. Sandstone-coloured tiles throughout made the place feel cooler. The large sliding glass doors at the back led out into an outdoor entertaining area as big as the house.

"You can put your stuff in the spare room. Do you want a drink?" Dean asked with his head in the fridge.

"Sounds good." She tossed her bags on the queen bed.

With a cold beer in hand, she made her way down the back stairs with Dean close behind. Her eyes scanned the lush tropical garden. A pizza oven and bar-b-que in one corner, an old snow-queen fridge against the wall and a spa in the other corner. All with a six-seater outdoor table in the middle under a sail of shade cloth. Dean put his drink on the table before placing his arm over her shoulder, "What do you think?"

"It's beautiful. Is the spa heated?"

"I don't know, it should work. It usually doesn't get cold enough for the heater." He grinned, "We will have to test it out later."

"How big is this place?"

"Come, I'll show you around," he drew her closer as he picked up this beer and they wandered down the garden path.

He picked a red hibiscus flower placing it behind her ear, "Now you look tropical."

"How long have you owned this place?"

"Just over a month," he pushed a dead palm frond off the path, "That big tour paid for most of it."

The path ended back at the front of the house. Heading back inside the air-conditioning was refreshing. Her stomach grumbled. *I didn't get lunch, a muffin on the plane doesn't count.* She looked at her phone. *Three PM.* "What are you planning for dinner? I missed lunch."

He grabbed a banana off the kitchen counter handing it to her,

"This should last you till dinner. Let's get some fish and chips and have dinner on the beach."

The sun slowly sank behind the hills. Away from the town, the beach was empty. They strolled along the open sands hand in hand. Her long blonde hair danced in the fresh sea breeze. The incoming tide lapped the shore.

Dean pointed to a flat area in the shade of the palms, "Let's have dinner over there."

Sitting on the rug, Dean handed her a cold beer. Raising his beer to hers, "Cheers." Taking a sip, his eyes connected with hers. Leaning towards her, "I missed you."

She moved closer, her gaze fixed on his cute smile. He gently slid his palm along her cheek, his touch was warm and gentle, she closed her eyes as his soft lips met hers.

"This place is beautiful." Looking out to sea, the sails on a distant yacht filled as they caught the wind. She took a bite of a chip, "What can we do here?"

"We can do anything. Forest walks, fishing, sailing, island hopping, snorkelling. You name it."

"But what do you do with your tour group?"

"Anything they want to pay me to organise."

She slapped at an irritating sting on the back of her neck. "Oh, yeah. Go downwind and shower in this," Dean handed her a tin of mosquito repellent.

Coughing from the repellent as she laid back on the rug, she turned to him, "Does this count as part of the week tour?"

He smiled, "Stay as long as you want."

"Well, I have two weeks."

He rolled over, looking down at her, "Plenty of time."

His soft lips caressed hers as another sting hit her arm. She slapped her forearm, "Let's test out that spa."

The water bubbled for about half an hour, Dean ran his hand through the water, "It will take all night to heat up."

Sonia dropped her robe, "Stuff it, I'm going in." The water was as cool as the rivers nearby.

He climbed in and sat across from her, his eyes gazing back at her, "Turn around."

Sitting with her back to him, his hands started to massage her shoulders. *Oh, I didn't know my muscles hurt that much.* She closed her eyes letting the tension drift away at his touch. After a while he reached around placing his arm across her waist, pulling her closer to his body. The touch of his fingers pushing her hair to the side as he nibbled her neck made her gasp.

It's day three, Dean got off the phone as Sonia prepared breakfast. "Want to go fishing on the dam today?"

"Sure. Do you have a boat?"

"No, a couple messaged me late last night and wanted a fishing day on the dam," he replied, "I have just booked the boat."

"Work? I can stay here."

He slid his arms around her waist, "I want you to come." Pausing as he looked back at her, "I have been thinking. Move up here, join me. I could do with a second person to help on the tours."

She looked back stunned. *Move up here?* "Wow, I'll have to think about it."

"OK." Grabbing his plate he reached for the food, "Eat up, we are meeting them at the dam in two hours." Taking a big bite of his toast he packed his day pack.

The dam level was high; most of the dead trees sat below the water line. Dean pulled up in his four-wheel drive, the skipper had the boat in the water. The two tourists were standing on the water's edge.

Dean loaded his gear in the boat, turning to load the tourist's equipment he paused before continuing. Returning to the car for more gear, "It's going to be a big day."

"Why?" Sonia reached for her hat.

"Their fishing gear is still in the shop packets with price tags hanging off it. I have to set it up first."

"That's what they are paying you for."

They were alone on the water, the bright sunshine blazed down from above, Sonia sat back with the skipper chatting. Dean was at the back of the boat giving the tourist lessons on using a fishing rod. *He looks so happy. Out in nature getting paid to explore and have fun.* Memories of her water rescue came back. *Well, it's not all fun. Every day is different from the last, hiking today, reef tomorrow. It sounds like an interesting job; I could see myself doing this.*

Later that evening Dean flipped the sausages on the bar-b-que. The smell of cooking food merged with the wafting smoke of smouldering mosquito-repellent coils. Sonia walked up beside him, her arm around his waist, "I have given work my four weeks' notice."

He glanced back at her, his eyes widening. "Really?" His face lit up.

"Yes. I will have to go back and finish up my work and organise the move."

Dropping the tongs on the table he threw his arms around her waist; his firm embrace lifted her feet off the ground. "This deserves a drink," he pulled a couple of beers from the outside fridge.

Another sunny day near Proserpine. Hand in hand they walked along the track to Cedar Creek Falls. The sound of running water filtered through the forest. Large rock beds and ferns surrounded the tropical pools at the bottom of the falls, still flowing strong from the wet season.

She stripped down to her bikini and stuck her toes in the pool.

The water was refreshingly cool. Paddling around, he wrapped his arms around her waist, "I don't know if I can wait four weeks."

Her arms around his neck, "Same here." Gliding her fingers through his wet hair, she leaned in for a long slow kiss.

Two weeks went by quickly. Back at the Mackay airport, the final call came to board the plane. She leaned over, "See you in three weeks."

"I will miss you."

"I will call when I get home."

The flight home was not as exciting as the trip up. Her thoughts were focused on what she needed to organise for the move. *I can get rid of my ski gear. And I will have to get some more summer clothes.*

The three weeks went fast, her days busy training her replacement and her evenings spent packing. Living out of a suitcase, she was surrounded by boxes. Getting out of bed on the last day, she jammed all the dirty bed linen in a bag as the removalist knocked on the door. *Well, that's it, goodbye to the old life, hello to a new life.*

Back at the Mackay airport, she was greeted with the same loving smile. But his greeting felt more permanent this time. The nerves and caution were gone. He reached out placing a camouflage-coloured cap on her head as he leaned in for a kiss. She removed the cap running her gaze over the logo. *D M Ford Tours.* "Part of the team now," he replied grabbing her luggage. There were more bags this time as it was all she had to live from until the removalist arrived.

Chilling that evening over dinner, he took hold of her hand, "We have a cruise tomorrow around the islands."

"A tour?"

"Yes. Ten Japanese tourists."

"Work on the first day. I can stay here and settle in."

He leaned in closer, "No. I can't leave you here while we are out having fun. I need your company."

She smiled leaning in with a kiss, "I better get some sleep tonight then."

The sun rises early in the tropics. After a quick breakfast, they made their way down to the marina. *The tourists were part of a group; lucky for us, they came with an interpreter.* Sonia leaned against the railing as the sea spray blew past, islands were visible on the horizon as the catamaran crashed through the waves. Warm sea breezes blew her hair everywhere; the crystal-clear water revealed a variety of sea creatures. Dean came up beside her, "How are you going?"

"I could get used to this."

The End of Story 4.

SHORT STORY 5

LOVE IN FLIGHT

Contemporary Christmas Workplace Romance

Written By C. L. Hamilton

C. L. Hamilton

5. LOVE IN FLIGHT

Plans make people think they are in control of their lives. The printer whirr blended with the Christmas Carols playing on the overhead speaker. Jemma sat at her desk madly typing as her phone alarm buzzed. *Yeah, I'm coming.* A warning popped up on the computer screen. *The printer is out of paper. Damn.* She was head down, thumping away at the printer drawer when Brendan stuck his head through the mine office doorway.

"How much longer are you going to be? The bus is ready to leave."

"Give me a minute," she replied hitting more printer buttons. *I will file them after Christmas.*

Scurrying across the mine carpark, Jemma was the last to arrive at the bus. On board, she scanned the crowd of workers heading home for the holidays looking for a seat. The only spot left was beside Brendan. Buckling up as the bus moved off, Jemma took a deep breath. *This is the first break I have had all day. I'm glad I completed the holiday pay schedule earlier in the week. It feels strange leaving work with the sun directly overhead. But everyone has flights to catch to be home in time for Christmas.*

"I saved you a spot," Brendan pulled out his travel mints. "Want one?" *His pleasant smile always lifted my mood.*

She smiled holding out her hand, "Thanks." *I wish the other workers were as nice as this guy. He is a keeper. It's a shame he is taken.*

The Briggsville airport was chaotic with the holiday rush. Jemma swung her backpack over her shoulder. She waved, giving her workmates a quick Merry Christmas as the mine bus pulled away from the footpath. *I better hurry up I don't want to miss the flight.* Brendan, the site manager who lived in the same town as her, had already disappeared into the bustle. *He will save me a spot in the line.*

Pushing through the crowds, the airline check-in area had people everywhere. *Where is the line? Where's Brendan?* Her eyes darted around trying to find him in amongst the rabble. He was off to the side leaning against a column flicking through his phone. *What is he doing over there?* She glanced up at the departure information board. *Flight cancelled! What? I have to find another flight.* Her shoulders dropped; she sighed as she joined the line of angry ticket holders queuing at the counter. *Where am I going to find a flight this close to Christmas?*

Brendan tapped her arm, " I booked us on the mail plane."

"Mail plane?" *Are we postage now?*

"It's all I can find. It ends in Newport after a few stops," he slipped his phone into his pocket, "We have to hurry, they are waiting for us."

Rushing while pushing past people and being shoved aside by others was tiring. Her feet ached from wearing the safety boots all day. *Why did the gate have to be at the other end of the airport?*

Arriving at the gate, Jemma looked at the flight information on the ticket, "Six hours, it's usually a two-hour flight?"

"They're delivering the mail to the remote towns," Brendan replied as he handed over his bag.

Being Christmas the plane will be packed with parcels. I hope there is space for us. Approaching the counter, she handed over her bag.

"Can you stand on the scales please," asked the booking officer.

Jemma raised her eyebrows, "Get on the scale?"

"It's a freight plane, they need to know their total weight for planning," Brendan stepped on the scales.

He's 97 kilograms. Her hands became sweaty. *I don't want him to know how much I weigh.* Jemma glanced back at him, "Turn around."

He shook his head as he turned to look out the window.

The pilot greeted them at the gate, and after a radio message, they made their way onto the tarmac. Before them a twin-engine eight-seater plane. *It looks small, I hope we all fit.* The back seats had been removed and replaced with boxes and cargo netting. Two seats sat directly behind the pilot, one on either side of the cockpit. After a safety briefing, they were off. The plane was loaded to the roof with mail making the take-off laboured.

The third town came over the horizon. They flew low over the trees lining up with a dirt track. A short bitumen runway was visible ahead. *Do we have to land on that?* The plane bounced on the first touchdown, coming down a second time. A loud twang resonated from the front of the cockpit. "Crap. The front gear," the pilot muttered as the plane nose dropped. The plane vibrated, and the grinding sound of metal on bitumen filled the air. With no steering, the nose swerved off the runway onto the grass. Jemma and Brendan were jerked forward bouncing off the seats in front.

Crap, he is trying to kill us. Jemma pushed back trying to sit up with the plane now resting at an angle.

"Is everyone all right?" The pilot asked.

"We will live," Jemma replied.

Brendan reached out his hand, "Are you OK?" She nodded taking hold of his hand as she tried to regain her balance on the sloping floor.

The pilot went back to muttering under his breath; flicking switches and pulling out his phone. "Get your gear, we aren't going anywhere today."

"But it's Christmas Eve. We have to get home," Jemma said.

"Yeah, well the office is closed and the other pilot is on holiday," the pilot replied as the airport fire truck arrived.

Jemma stood in the plane doorway looking at the stairs partly extending at an angle. *How am I going to get out of this?*

"Here, let me," Brendan pushed past her jumping onto the ground. Holding up his arms he said, "Jump."

She froze. *He can't catch me.*

"Come on."

Taking a big breath she took a leap of faith. He grabbed the sides of her chest as her hands gripped his shoulders. On the ground and in his arms, her muscles tightened as her heart thumped in her chest.

Her hands slowly slid down his arms as she stepped back, "Thanks."

The sun hung low on the horizon as the shadows crept across the airport field. Jemma turned towards Brendan, "Where are we staying tonight?"

"We will find something," he replied as they walked across the tarmac toward the airport.

They arrived at the only hotel in town. The partying had started with cheering coming from the next room. The receptionist asked their names, "Brendan Kennedy."

The receptionist looked up from the computer, "I don't have a booking in that name."

"We were on the damaged mail plane. Do you know where we can get a room?" Jemma leaned over the counter.

"We are booked out for Christmas." The receptionist paused looking over her shoulder, "I have a spare room over my garage next door."

"Anything will do," Jemma sighed as she grabbed her bag.

"Should I book you a table for dinner?"

"Yes please," Brendan replied.

"See you at seven o'clock."

The last of the daylight was dwindling. Jemma looked into the dark gap between the buildings. *The entrance is at the back of the alley. Every crime novel starts this way. Couldn't they afford a light?*

"You can go first," Jemma pointed into the darkness.

Walking single file down the passageway beside the hotel they reached a set of stairs. Opening the door, Jemma froze. She scanned the single room to see a double bed, a lounge chair, a television and an ensuite in the corner. "There is only one bed."

Brendan dropped his bag on the couch, "I can sleep here. You have the bed."

She looked down at the two-seater lounge, "That's too short for you."

"Well, it's too short for you too. I will sleep on the floor if I have to." He said, "You know me, I'll sleep anywhere."

I can't have him sleeping on the hard floor. And I will trip over him going to the bathroom. Her pulse increased, and she took a deep breath. "We can share the bed. I will just have to control myself," she smiled to hide her nerves.

"Take the fun out of it," he grinned. "I'm going for a shower before dinner."

Jemma grabbed her phone, "Good idea. I will ring my parents; they will be expecting me." She was lying on the bed chatting on the phone when Brendan came out wearing nothing but a towel wrapped low around his hips. His bare sculptured chest broke her train of thought. Stopping mid-sentence her eyes tracked him across the room. *Did he forget his clothes?* He sat on the edge of the bed silently looking back at her. Her pulse jumped.

"I have to go, I'll ring you later," Jemma said sitting up. *What is his problem?* Her eyes locked on his; she raised an eyebrow. "What's up?"

"Can you check my back? I had my stitches removed two days ago," he turned with his back to her, "I want to make sure that landing didn't do anything."

She held her breath as she leaned forward, her eyes slowly perused his broad shoulders moving down to a red scar in the middle of his back. "Looks fine to me." She replied moving back.

"Cool," he returned to the bathroom.

Her eyes followed him through the doorway. Once the bathroom door was closed, she let out a big gasp. She took several deep breaths to calm her nerves.

Arriving at the restaurant the waiter looked up from the booking list, "Mr and Mrs Kennedy. Follow me."

Jemma's eyes widened glancing at Brendan. "We are married?"

"You wish," he replied with a smirk.

"Well, don't tell your wife," Jemma murmured.

Brendan pulled back her seat, leaned over her shoulder and whispered, "I don't have a wife."

What? His file said he was married. Have they split up? The thought of him being single and spending the night sharing a bed made her stomach knot.

The table was covered in Christmas decorations and candles flickering in glass jars. She looked across at a guy she barely knew personally but wanted to know better. *A first date when we aren't dating seems weird.* This was the first time she had sat back and looked at him up closely. His short brown hair, warm hazel eyes, the late afternoon stubble on his square jaw and soft smile were alluring.

The waiter placed a bottle of wine on the table with two glasses. Jemma looked back at Brendan, "We didn't order wine."

"Merry Christmas. I got us in this mess, it's the least I can do," he replied picking up the bottle.

"Talking of messes. How are we going to get home?"

"I'll have to find the pilot and work that out," he replied, filling her glass.

The Christmas buffet was loaded with roasts, vegetables, seafood, and salad, the trays went on and on. Jemma scanned the banquet. *It was easier at the mine. Choose beef or chicken.* There was not much talking over dinner. *What do you say to management? He's not my boss but he is in the team.* She placed her fork on the plate, taking her last sip of wine.

"What were your plans for tonight? Before the plane crashed," she asked.

"Just a quiet night at home with my dogs. Ring my sister at some point," he replied, "And yourself."

"Dinner with my parents, nothing fancy."

The sound of billiard balls smashing together and someone cheering caught Brendan's attention. His face lit up as he looked back at Jemma, "Want a game of pool?"

"Do you want me to beat you again?" She asked.

"That was the dodgy table at the mine. It's not level."

Gathering their drinks they moved over near the pool tables waiting for their turn. They started talking to another couple waiting for a game. With the last ball pocketed, the other bloke asked, "Do you and your wife want to have a doubles game?"

"She isn't my wife," Brendan replied.

"Sorry, girlfriend."

Jemma grabbed a triangle frame and reached into the pocket. *I give up. Married, no girlfriend what the?*

Partway through the game, the pilot walked over to Brendan, "A new plane will be here at six tomorrow morning to pick us up."

Six, another early morning. She stood back with her cue in hand watching Brendan reaching over the table. *Does he have a girlfriend? He doesn't give much away. It's like he enjoys tensing me.*

Brendan pocketed the last ball, "That will do. We have an early morning."

Back in their room, Jemma turned on the kettle as Brendan sat on the lounge flicking through the TV channels. Endless Christmas carols and old movies. He flicked the TV off as Jemma asked, "Do you want a cuppa?"

"Tea would be nice."

She approached the lounge, handing him his cup. "I enjoyed tonight." Taking a seat beside him, their bodies only inches apart on the small lounge.

"Yes. I won the Pool game," he chuckled.

"We were on the same team," she sipped her coffee.

He flicked over his phone before putting it back on the coffee table, "Is this how you thought you would spend Christmas?"

"No. We have been taking the same flight to work and back each week for the last four years with no big problems," she said. "We take one mail plane and we are sleeping together."

He turned his head, cocking an eyebrow, "This is hardly sleeping together. You have slept closer to me on the airline."

"When?" She straightened her back.

"Last year. You know when the flight got delayed three hours," he replied. "You fell asleep with your head on my shoulder."

"I don't remember that." Looking over her cup her eyes fixed on his face trying to read his body language. "Why does everyone think we are married?"

"I don't know. Maybe we look the part."

How do married couples look? She shuffled in her seat. "Can I ask a personal question?"

He turned towards her, folding one leg under the other. Resting one hand on the back of the seat, his gaze connected with hers, "What do you want to know?"

"In the restaurant, you said you didn't have a wife," she paused, "I thought you were married."

"No. That was years ago. She didn't like me being away at the mine and found someone else."

"I'm sorry I shouldn't have asked," Jemma looked away to her cup.

"Don't worry about it. Anyone in your life?"

"No. I have received a few proposals at work," she shrugged her shoulders while screwing up her face, "But hell no." *I didn't need that memory returning.*

"So, you're not into anyone at work?" He asked gazing deeply into her eyes.

She looked back with a coy smile and didn't say anything.

"I see." He stretched and yawned, "Well, I'm going to bed."

"I'll be over later." She sipped her coffee, staring at the black TV screen while organising her thoughts.

From the corner of her eye, she caught a glimpse of Brendan pulling his shirt off showing that chest again.

Beads of sweat started to form on her brow as her chest tightened. *Oh, boy.* "Tell me you sleep with your clothes on."

"I will tonight," he said removing his pants and climbing into bed wearing his boxer shorts.

Boxers, well that does count as clothing. She went back to her cup of coffee.

The alarm went off, and Jemma awoke to Brendan packing his bag wearing nothing but the towel again. *Wow, doesn't he like wearing clothes?* Trying to ignore the view, she sat up in bed looking out the window at the hotel next door.

"Good morning, your coffee is on your side table."

Coffee too? I could do a lot worse than this guy. She pulled out her phone trying to focus on her emails while he worked on getting dressed.

They both stood in the airport field as the sun rose over the horizon, Brendan scanned the sky for the new plane. Jemma hung up her phone as she approached him. "Merry Christmas."

"Merry Christmas," he returned with a warm smile.

The new plane landed smoother than our flight. It pulled up near the broken plane jacked up on a trailer. After loading the mail, the new pilot came over, "Mr and Mrs Kennedy?"

"We are not married," Jemma said climbing on board.

"It's on the booking manifest," the new pilot replied.

"We work together, that's all," Jemma reached for her seat buckle.

The old pilot sat beside the new pilot, looking over the seat to Jemma, "You two act more like a couple than some of the couples I have travelled with."

"What makes you think that?"

"Couples move as one. They have their routine and know what the other is thinking," the old pilot said.

"Do we do that?"

"Yep," he replied turning around to tighten his seat belt.

Have we been travelling and working together that long that we move as one? She glanced sideways at Brendan who was reading the safety card. *The whole we are married theory doesn't seem to faze him. I just don't want to deal with the rumours at work.*

Finally touching down in Newport, getting their luggage from the mail plane was much quicker than a traditional airline. They stopped at the taxi rank out the front of the airport. "Do you have a lift home?" Jemma asked.

"Yeah, my car is in long-term parking," he pulled his car keys from his bag, "Do you want me to drop you home?"

"It's out of your way. I'll get a taxi."

"OK, Merry Christmas," he said leaning forward and kissing her cheek. "See you at next week."

Her heart skipped a beat. "Merry Christmas," she said stepping towards the next taxi in line.

She gazed out the taxi window at the passing cityscape. *Are there rules about management kissing staff on the cheek? It is Christmas, he was just being nice.*

The Christmas holiday didn't last long as the new work week started like the others, getting out of the taxi at the airport. She was late to book in, so Brendan ended up sitting in a different aisle for the flight. Meeting up as they climbed aboard the bus to the mine; he was back to being the serious manager. She shuffled down to the only empty seat left; Brendan briefly smiled at her as she passed.

Back in the office, another admin asked about her Christmas. "Pretty quiet, just the usual." The pile of filing left before Christmas kept her busy. Brendan dropped in occasionally to arrange paperwork. By the end of the week, Jemma was exhausted. The twelve-hour shifts had worn her down.

Brendan met up with her on the path to the carpark. "I was coming to get you."

"I'm here."

At the airport, they waited in line to check-in. Brendan leaned over, "We should have booked the mail plane."

She turned her head, "What the hell for?"

"I want to take you out to dinner again," he said casually looking ahead.

What did he say? Her eyes widened, and her neck stiffened as she looked back at him, "Dinner?"

"Yes. Dinner." He turned towards her, "What are you doing tomorrow night?"

"Sorry, I'm out of town this week visiting my folks," she murmured, "I get back Thursday night."

"Bugger, that's a shame, coffee on the way home then."

Standing outside the Newtown airport Jemma dropped her bag at her feet. "Where do you want to catch up for coffee?"

"Why don't I give you a lift home? We can stop off at a café along the way."

The multiple-storey carpark elevator doors opened to a sea of cars waiting for their masters to return. Brendan turned to the left pushing a button on his key fob. *A standard red sedan, it has seen a few years.*

"Not what I pictured a manager driving," Jemma said climbing in the passenger seat.

"I'm only a site manager. Not the company CEO."

Slowly winding down the spiral concrete ramp to the carpark exit, the walls were lined with scrap marks. *I wouldn't want to drive a large car in this place.* Cruising through the traffic, he pulled into a small café. They had a choice of outdoor tables and chairs set for two, hidden among the gardens.

The sun had disappeared over the horizon; the glow of the

streetlights replaced the dim twilight. They were both hungry as they had not had dinner. Coffee became a burger and chips laced with the romance of high-vis mining attire. His hair had become a bit ratty, but she still got a smile from his tired face. *I probably don't look any better.*

She held up her soft drink, "Cheers."

"Cheers," he replied, "This is not quite what I had planned for our dinner."

"What was your plan?"

He paused glancing up from the table, "Something nice at a restaurant, after a shower and looking better than this." He looked down at his yellow shirt scuffed with stains.

"It's the thought that counts."

With the last chip gone, Jemma arched her back, her muscles felt heavy, and her feet ached, "I need a bath and get out of these bloody boots."

He pulled up at the front of her apartment building, "See you next week."

She unbuckled her seat belt, leaned over and gave him a quick kiss on his cheek, "Thanks for dinner."

As she went to turn away, "Hey, before I forget," he said.

She turned back coming face to face with him. He tilted his head moving closer. She held her breath as a lump grew in her throat. His soft lips felt warm against hers. "Good night," he whispered.

"Good night."

Standing on the footpath she watched his taxi merge into the sea of tail lights. Her thoughts were reliving the last few moments. *He is getting serious.*

Jemma scanned the line of people boarding the flight. *Where is he?* Shuffling along towards the gate her eyes moving around the crowd.

Taking a seat, she couldn't see him. *He missed the flight. Did he catch another flight?*

Arriving at the mine office, everything was running as usual. The manager was on the phone all morning. One of the mine electricians came to the reception asking if anyone had seen Brendan. *He's not here?* Jemma dialled his mobile number but it rang out. Dialling several times achieved the same result. She checked the staff login sheets. *He didn't sign in.* Her chest started to tighten as she knocked on the manager's door. "Have you seen Brendan; a crew is asking for him."

"No. He is not answering."

What happened to him? Why hasn't he reported in? She tried his phone a few more times during the day with no luck.

Later that afternoon, her manager walked up to the reception counter, "Brendan was in a car accident on the way to the airport. He rang from the hospital; he won't be out this week." He said, "Erik will be stepping up until Brendan returns."

Accident! Her pulse raced, "Is he OK? What happened?"

"Dislocated shoulder and some abdominal bruising. They were keeping him in overnight for observation."

"I tried ringing his mobile and he didn't answer," Jemma said.

"He rang from the hospital phone. He may not have his mobile."

The following afternoon, the office phone rang. Jemma had her hands full filing paperwork when she wedged the phone under her ear. She stopped everything mid-task at the sound of Brendan's voice. A crew were chatting at the counter and office noise made it difficult to concentrate. "Brendan, I'll switch you to the meeting room, it is quieter."

Rushing into the room, shutting the door behind her, she took a deep breath and picked up the phone. "Brendan, are you all right?"

"Yeah, a sore shoulder and some bruised ribs. An idiot ran into me at the traffic lights and wrote off my car."

"Crap. At least you're alive." Her voice softened, "I rang your mobile several times. You had me worried."

"All my gear got carted away with the tow truck. The holding yard is near the airport," he groaned, "I haven't been able to get my phone back yet."

"I can get it on Friday and bring it to you," she said. "Where are you staying?"

"Home. I'll ring the depot and tell them you're coming," he replied, "Don't worry if you can't get it."

Friday evening, Jemma pulled up in front of Brendan's place. A young blonde woman climbed out of the car in his driveway and knocked on his door. He greeted her with a warm smile before she entered. Jemma sat in her car looking back at the door closing. *Who is she? Should I disturb them?* Sitting in the dark, her stomach grumbled. *I'm hungry. Damn it, it's been a long day.* She grabbed his kit bag and quietly placed it on the front steps before leaving.

The following morning, she was out shopping. *I need a coffee.* She grabbed a seat at a nearby outdoor café. While waiting for her order, she watched some birds raiding the leftovers at the next table. A car pulled up in front of the medical centre next door. Brendan clambered out of the passenger seat. *Brendan.* Jemma went to stand when she saw the same blonde woman climb out of the driver's seat and follow him into the clinic.

Her heart sank as she turned away. *Why did he ask me to dinner if he had a girlfriend?* The waiter approached, she reached out and tapped his arm, "Can I get my coffee takeaway?"

As the week went on, Jemma kept herself busy keeping her mind off Brendan. Packing her bag for work, she changed her ticket to an earlier flight. The flight and bus trip were quiet travelling by herself.

She arrived at the office shortly after sunrise, "You're early," the boss said.

"I have to catch up on the end-of-month reports," she replied.

The morning noise level increased when her usual bus load of workers arrived. Her eyes caught Brendan stepping off the bus. His arm was in a sling, he headed for the office. *I don't want to talk to him.* She got up and left for the bathroom.

Later that evening, Jemma sat on her front porch wrapped in a bathrobe drying her hair. She leaned back in her chair relaxing as she watched the sunset in the hills. The external lamps slowly lit up as the darkness crept in.

"Found you," came a voice from the darkness. Brendan stepped up to her stairs.

The lamp lit up his face. She glanced back, "Hi."

"Missed you on the flight this morning," he paused as she sat silent. "Is everything all right?"

"Yeah, I'm fine."

His gaze didn't move as he placed one foot on the bottom step before stopping, "Can I join you?"

She stared back at him, stone-faced. "Yeah." *This will be good.*

He brushed the dust off the spare seat before sitting, "Thanks, for dropping my gear off. Why didn't you knock? I was home."

"Your girlfriend arrived just as I got there, so I left your gear on the porch," she looked out at the bugs flying around the lamp.

"What girlfriend?" He leaned over the table trying to get her attention.

"How many girlfriends does he have?" She asked abruptly. "The young thin blonde one that visited you that same night."

"Oh, Megan." He straightened his back, "She's my dog walker who looks after my dogs during my work week. She drops by on Friday nights after I get paid to collect her wage."

"I saw you both at the doctor the following morning."

110

"I haven't got a car, she offered to drop me off and pick me up." He pulled his seat around facing Jemma, "Did you think she was my girlfriend?"

"I don't know what you do in your private life." Tears welled in her eyes as they connected with his. Her feelings of betrayal were being replaced with feeling foolish.

"Hell no, she is flat out being twenty. That's too young." He reached out placing his good hand on Jemma's knee, "I waited for your call, only to find my gear on the porch." He looked back, "Why didn't you call?"

Her eyes scanned the mining camp, some workers were jogging and others wandered around. *There are too many people about.* "Let's go inside. Do you want a coffee?"

"Water will be fine."

Sitting at the table she passed him his glass, "I didn't call as I don't have your number."

"You found my address on the work computer."

"That was at work. The only number you have on your file is your mobile. And that was at the tow shop," said replied, "Why didn't you call me?"

"Your number was on my mobile," his voice faded.

She dropped her head, taking a deep breath she looked back, "I'm sorry. The last couple of weeks have been stressful."

He stood up, stepping towards her with his arm outstretched, "I'm sorry I should have rung the office more." She wrapped her arms around his chest. "Not too tight," he groaned.

Crap. Pulling back, "Are your ribs still sore?"

"A little. My shoulder hurts more," he looked at the clock on the wall, "That reminds me I have to take my tablets."

Heading for the door, she said, "See you tomorrow."

"Yes, good night," he leaned forward and gently kissed her forehead. "Blondes are not my thing. I prefer brunettes," he flicked her brown hair with his fingers before turning for the door.

Standing in the doorway she smiled as he disappeared from the lamp light. Closing the door, she reached up touching the lock of hair he had just flicked. *Brunettes. We have to keep this professional at work.*

Another week over, Jemma stepped off the bus at the airport, grabbing her bag from the back as she said goodbye to another admin worker. Turning towards the airport entrance her eyes were drawn to Brendan standing at the doors. *He waited.* Together they approached the ticket counter when Brendan tapped her arm, "Wrong line," he said heading for the express check-in.

"But—"

"I upgraded us to Business Class. The seats are wider for my shoulder."

Business class. "I could have kept my original seat."

"I want someone interesting to talk to during the flight," he said placing his bag on the conveyor, "I don't want to be stuck with a businessman more interested in his share price."

Jemma headed for the usual gate when Brendan blocked her path. "We have two hours. Want to get something to eat in the business lounge?"

"Business lounge? Sure," she looked down at her high-vis work clothes and boots, "Should we not look like we are here to fix the plumbing?"

"Good idea."

"Damn," she grabbed his arm, "Our clothes have been checked into the luggage."

"Well, we will just have to buy some more." He replied heading towards the nearest retail shop.

In the toilet cubicle, Jemma squirmed trying to get changed. She cursed under her breath when she whacked her elbow into the wall pulling off her shirt. With the old clothes shoved in the shopping back, she adjusted her day dress before slipping her sandals onto her tired aching feet. *I'm glad to get those boots off.* Pulling out her hair tie she flicked her head to make her hair fall over her shoulders. Arriving back at the lounge, Brendan was in jeans, a button-up shirt and on his phone, hanging up as she approached.

"You look good," he said.

"So do you."

"I could have used your help getting my shirt over my stuffed shoulder."

She smiled back, her cheeks reddening as memories of him shirtless at Christmas flashed before her eyes.

The glass doors opened into another world. A full coffee bar with twenty different flavours of beans. Food buffet, computer terminals and lounges hidden away behind large TVs. Stepping forward, they showed their tickets to the receptionist. Brendan asked for a bottle of red and cheese platter before they moved to a corner suite.

Jemma sat quietly scanning the room, her arms tucked tight to her side. Suits everywhere with their faces buried in their laptops. *I should have bought a more expensive outfit.* The only thing comforting her was that they were self-absorbed in their little world.

Brendan eased down beside her, "What's up? You seem uncomfortable."

"I have never been in here before. It feels like I shouldn't be here."

He slid closer, taking hold of her hand, "This is just a quiet area for the bosses to keep ordering their employees around over the internet." He panned the room, "Look at them, not a smile in the place."

"Why are we here then?"

"To enjoy ourselves. Get to know each other in a place where the staff don't ask questions."

Her eyes ran up his chest, connecting with his gaze. Their interaction was broken when the waiter placed their order on the coffee table. While the waiter poured wine into their glasses he asked, "Is there anything else."

"No, thank you," Brendan replied handing Jemma her drink.

"So, how was your week?" She asked.

"Not great. A trainee ran over the pressure hose and someone special was upset about me having a mythical girlfriend." He sipped his wine, "But I sorted out both problems."

"I'm glad you did." Her phone buzzed. *Ten-minute warning.* That hour went quickly. She grabbed the last olive off the plate as she rose. Brendan with only one arm struggled to pull himself out of the low lounge. She took his hand and hauled him to his feet.

The plane started to descend as they neared Newport. Jemma stared out the aeroplane window to the clouds below. Brendan leaned over her shoulder, "Can you drop me home? I rang Megan before we left saying I didn't need a lift."

She glanced back and nodded, "Sure. We will take the taxi home to get my car." Taking a moment, she whispered, "Why don't you stay at my place tonight?"

He took hold of her hand, "Are you sure? He asked in a quiet smooth voice. "You're welcome to stay at my place. It's quieter than the city."

Her pulse increased, her eyes locking with his. She entwined her fingers with his and lightly squeezed his palm. *Business class is no place for a kiss.*

After a quick car change, she didn't need directions to his house as she pulled up in his driveway. Opening the front door, he placed his bag on the floor before sliding her bag off her shoulder and placing it next to his. "Welcome to my digs. What would you like for dinner?"

"Whatever you're having." She scanned the room. *Modern and clean, an upgrade from my one-bed apartment.* "Where are your dogs?"

He leaned against the kitchen bench, head down typing on his phone, "At Megan's. When I rang earlier, I told her we would pick them up tomorrow."

"OK, do I have time for a shower before dinner?"

"Sure, down the hall on the right."

She wrapped her wet hair in a towel and dug into the work bag. *What am I going to wear?* Pulling out her pyjamas. *No way.* She looked back at the dress she bought at the airport. That's the best outfit I have. *Why didn't I get some clothes when I picked up my car?* After some perfume, she gathered her things.

He passed her in the hall, "Takeaway shouldn't be long. I'll grab a quick shower before it gets here."

Stepping into the living room, Jemma's eyes open wide. The dining table was set up for a dinner for two. *A bottle of wine, glasses, and cutlery. Who has a takeaway meal like this?*

"Jemma, have you got a minute?" He called down the hall. She turned around to see him standing behind her with his shirt unbuttoned. The ripples in the open shirt followed the muscles peeking out underneath. "Can you help me get my shirt off?"

Her heart skipped a beat as she stepped forward, each slow breath drawing him nearer. Placing her hands over his heart. Her fingers were inside his shirt, slowly gliding over his chest towards his shoulders. The feeling of goosebumps rising on his skin. Her touch guided the sleeve down his good arm. She reached around to remove the last sleeve; his skin was warm next to hers. He ran his fingers under her jaw and lifted her face, those hazel eyes trapping her gaze.

Moving in closer, she closed her eyes as his tender lips met hers. No one noticed his shirt falling to the floor. He slowly stepped back, "I'm meant to be having a shower."

She fought off a smile as he turned back to the bathroom. *I could have helped him undress all week.* Flopping down in the lounge she took a couple of slow deep breaths. Her insides tingled as she focused on getting her heart rate down. The doorbell ringing drew her thoughts back into the room.

As she placed the Chinese food on the table Brendan's voice came from behind, "Good dinner is here." Glancing over her shoulder, he was dressed in the same attire he wore in the room Christmas Eve, bare-chested with a towel around his hips. *Tempting, but let's be civilised during dinner.*

"Are you going to get dressed first?"

"Yeah," he replied heading into the bedroom returning moments later wearing a pair of tracksuit pants low on his hips and a white cotton shirt with every button undone.

An unbuttoned shirt. He must have liked the way I removed it last time. Don't get distracted. Dinner time. She sat at the table, "Where's your sling?"

"My shoulder is getting better. Wearing the sling at work and during the flight gets me privileges." He smiled as he sat down.

"And it's an excuse to have women undress you."

"Women? There has only been you." He said straight-faced pausing before returning a cheeky grin, "I didn't hear you complain."

Feeling her cheeks redden, she lowered her face. Her eyes turned back as she attempted to cover her smile with her hand.

Pouring her a glass of wine, he raised his glass, "Merry Christmas."

Lifting her glass, "Christmas?" *A bit late for that.*

"This is how we should have spent Christmas," his eyes stared back as he leaned towards her ending with a sweet kiss.

Her heart was pounding. She moved back, "Merry Christmas," she whispered.

"If it weren't for that mail plane incident we would be eating alone tonight," he said.

Now who's taking the fun out of it? "And travelling to work and back together each week and hiding our true feelings for each other," she replied.

"We were always in the public realm, we never had the chance to be alone together," he said cleaning up dinner. "I never knew what you were thinking."

She carried the dishes to the sink, "I thought you were married."

The fridge door closed; Brendan stepped up behind Jemma placing his hands around her waist, "Don't worry about the dishes. Let's move to the lounge and relax."

Sitting at the far end of the couch, she sipped her wine. Her eyes tracked him across the room as he sat down. He slid closer placing his arm on the headrest behind her, "I missed you. The week of my accident and when I didn't see you drop off my bag," he said. "It was a hard fortnight; I needed a friendly face."

"I didn't know. I was worried when you didn't show up at the airport," she said.

"Let's make sure that never happens again," he replied moving closer lowering his arm over her shoulders and drawing her closer. His shirt fell by the side of his body hiding nothing. She gently leaned against his bare chest, draping her arm over his waist. His cologne lightly masked his alluring manly scent. As her nerves eased, she murmured, "These last few weeks have been a mess." She closed her eyes taking a long slow breath.

Sitting silently together, arm in arm her thoughts were going over the past few months. The feelings she had when they were forced together on Christmas Eve, his accident and how he had opened up about his feelings toward her. She blankly stared across his chest, each hair contouring the muscles beneath. Lightly drawing her fingers along his ribs, she whispered, "You know I have seen you almost naked more times than we have kissed."

"We will have to fix that," his voice was deep and smooth as he leaned forward. His hand slid along her jaw as he gently lifted her head. A shiver ran up her spine, as his tender lips caressed hers in a slow kiss. His electric touch made the hairs on her body rise. Her fingers ran through his soft hair.

After a week of getting to know him well, Jemma looked back at Brendan from the passenger seat as he pulled into his long-term airport carpark in his new car. She unbuckled and reached for the door handle. "Just a minute," Brendan said reaching behind the seat. In his hand a gift-wrapped rectangular box.

Her eyes widened as she looked at the gift and then at his smile. "What's this?"

"Late Valentine's present."

I didn't get him anything. Peeling back the wrapper, a gold dress watch lay in her hand. She reached out with a loving kiss, "Thank you."

"The mine has a no jewellery policy but you are allowed to wear a watch," he said. "Something to remember me by when I'm not around."

She reached over showing her affection with another kiss.

Brendan sat back, "While this is great, we don't want to miss the flight."

The End of Story 5.

ABOUT THE AUTHOR

Christine L. Hamilton enjoys writing short stories and novels in the genre of Sci-fi, and Adventure with a romantic subplot. As well as Contemporary Romance works, written to Sweet Romance to closed-door heat level. Currently self-employed as a freelance writer, she creates a range of fiction and non-fiction books. She grew up in outback Queensland Australia and now lives in tropical north Queensland. Living in rural Australia and her twenty-seven-year career in the emergency services gave her a different look at life events which she includes in her story plots. Her works can be found at www.pagesnmore.com.

I hope you enjoyed this book, please leave a review to help others when choosing this book. Thank you.

www.ingramcontent.com/pod-product-compliance
Lightning Source LLC
Chambersburg PA
CBHW022033170626
46808CB00003B/1183